AGAINST THE WIND

Book 2 in the Agents of the Crown Trilogy

Regan Walker

"A fabulous tale with exciting twists and turns reflecting a little-known event in England's history, and at its heart…a wonderful love story."

—*New York Times* Best-selling Author Shirlee Busbee

A RISING STORM

"Is making love something you do not wish to do?" he said. "As I recall, you seemed to enjoy it as much as I did." Then, more tenderly: "Besides, I have missed you, Kitten."

"No…I cannot. I am not your…your…" She could not bring herself to say the word. Their one night together had been a wonderful, amazing, and yes, passionate experience, but it could never happen again. She had escaped for one dreadful night into a dream. Into his arms. As much as she wanted those around her again, wanted to lie with him, she could not allow it. This was not who she was. Not who she was raised to be.

Placing his hands on her waist, he pulled her against him. The heat from his broad chest overwhelmed her as she stared into indigo eyes now stormy with desire. "You opened a door, Kitten, I'm unwilling to close."

AGAINST THE WIND

Book 2 in the Agents of the Crown Trilogy

Regan Walker

www.BOROUGHSPUBLISHINGGROUP.com

AGAINST THE WIND
Copyright © 2013 Regan Walker

Digital edition created by Maureen Cutajar
www.gopublished.com

ISBN 978-1-941260-21-0

Contents

Prologue

Paris, 1812

Sir Martin Powell dragged his fingers through his hair and poured himself a glass of brandy, the only luxury his small office afforded. Though he loved his work and never questioned his duty to the Crown, the last few days had not been pleasant.

For days he'd watched the soldiers stumble into Paris from the Russian warfront, gaunt, pale men, their uniforms in tatters and their faces reflecting the gruesome deaths they witnessed. Many more—hundreds of thousands from Napoleon's *Grande Armée*— would never be coming home. Though almost all of England would rejoice, the slaughter sickened Martin. But the Crown expected him to wait and watch. And to send reports of all he observed.

It was nearly Christmas, and to cheer his wife Elise he'd promised a drink to celebrate with their good friend Ormond, another Englishman serving the Prince Regent through espionage in France. Martin hated to be late for anything, so he hastily finished his brandy, shoved back his chair and grabbed his coat. An hour later the three were seated in their favorite café, crowded and noisy on this frosty December night. All around, returning soldiers sought solace in drink. Martin scanned the room, studying the men's faces. After all these years it was second nature to be aware of those he might have to face in a skirmish, their weapons, and the exits he might need for escape.

Tossing back her head of dark curls, Elise laughed at something Ormond said. The sound always reminded Martin of bells tinkling. How he loved her smile, so openly displaying her love of life. He had married her too young, he knew, and it had been taking a serious risk given his situation, but one day he would return to England and he wanted Elise with him. She was like a fresh wind off the sea, a soothing balm to his oft-troubled soul.

As they always did in public, they spoke in French.

"I understand there is more to celebrate tonight than Christmas, my good friend." Ormond followed these words with a wink.

"You told him?" Martin asked, turning to face his wife and seeing her mischievous smile.

"*Oui*, I did. Ormond is like a brother; I could not keep it from him. He was happy to share our joy."

She beamed, and Martin could not be angry. Elise was right. His colleague and good friend did need to know, and Martin was pleased as well, though he was reticent to bring a child into the world during a time of war.

"Since we've shared the news, let's share a toast to the babe!" exclaimed Ormond, calling for champagne. Soon their three glasses were raised in celebration. "What are you wanting, you two? A boy or a girl?"

"I am hoping for a boy—for Martin," Elise said. "One with his blue eyes."

"And I will take whatever you give me, my love," Martin reminded her, leaning over to bestow a kiss that brought a smile to her sweet face and to him a feeling of contentment. He'd known little enough of it until the day she came into his life.

Downing the last of his drink, Martin kissed his young wife again on the cheek and the three rose to leave. There was much yet to do.

The night air was wintry as they exited the crowded café. The cold felt good, invigorating. Martin had just taken a deep breath when several soldiers emerged from the café behind him, swearing and complaining amongst themselves about Napoleon deserting his troops in his haste to return to Paris. One of them was defending his emperor. The men were drunk, angry and looking for a fight. The warning sounded in Martin's head, but this was a night for celebration, not war, so he shrugged and walked on, his hand under Elise's elbow.

Suddenly, out of the corner of his eye, he saw a brandished pistol. A man shouted, followed by an explosive shot, and Elise slumped to the ground. In the light from the tavern Martin saw a circle of blood widening on her chest.

"Elise!" he cried, dropping to his knees beside his wife. "*Dieu, no. Mon amour.*"

A terrible anger filled his soul like a gathering storm. Maddened, he rose and spun, pulling his knife. He struck out toward the throat of the man who had fired the pistol. The soldier was an easy target, too stunned by what he had done to move, but before Martin's blade could fall the two other soldiers attacked him, one swinging a fist into Martin's ribs and the other holding a knife to his throat.

Instantly Ormond was there. He leveled a pistol on the soldiers. *"Laissez-le aller!"*

Seeing the weapon, the soldiers let Martin go. Though he fired no shot, Ormond's pistol never wavered and the soldiers fled into the night.

Martin reached for his wife, taking her into his arms. He cradled her close to his chest as he rocked back and forth, saying her name over and over. "Elise…Elise…Elise…."

Ormond knelt beside him, wrapping an arm around his shoulders. Martin felt his friend's touch, but there was no comfort to be had. There was no bringing back the girl whose vacant brown eyes stared up at him.

However, there was apparently another function that certain of the deaf servants carried out – they were used in the Ottoman Court as killers or executors! They were said to be physically powerful men, handy with a bowstring. From time to time, the Ottoman ruler might wish to remove one or two of his officials or family members. Sometimes the Sultan obtained legal and religious permission for the deaths, which was effected by official executioners who were not deaf. In other cases, especially where the Sultan wished to avoid publicity, he might simply give the 'nod' to the deaf servants on duty and they would carry out the murder or assassination with a bowstring. Because they were powerful men, the victim often didn't have a prayer. Bowstrings were especially suitable for royal persons, as they did not spill any blood.

In 1553 and 1554, the Ottoman Empire was fighting many battles in the Nahcivan region (in what is now modern-day Azerbaijan), and Sultan Süleyman travelled forth with his army and entourage from Istanbul, including many members of his court, to meet up with the army commanded by his eldest (and strongest) son, Prince Mustapha.

Before he left Istanbul, Sultan Süleyman had a session with his favourite wife, Hürrem Sultan, who persuaded him that Prince Mustapha wanted his father killed so that he could become Sultan. In reality, Hürrem Sultan wanted her own son Selim, who also happened to be Sultan Süleyman's favourite son, to become Sultan on the death of his father and had plotted to get rid of Prince Mustapha.

Hürrem Sultan, favourite wife of
Sultan Süleyman

When the two armies met up ay Konya in central Turkey, the Sultan's travelling tents were erected and Prince Mustapha was installed in one of the inner tents belonging to his father. According to a detailed report that survives of the incident, as soon as Prince Mustapha entered the inner tent, he was set upon by a group of Sultan Süleyman's deaf servants who endeavoured to put the fatal bowstring noose around Mustapha's neck.

However, Prince Mustapha was a man of considerable strength and fought back valiantly. Separated by only a thin linen hanging from the inner tent where the struggle was being carried out, Sultan Süleyman could not help but overhear what was going on, and irked at the unexpected delay in the execution of the murder, he stuck his head out of his own chamber and glared at his deaf servants, and at the same time, he signed to them urging them to hurry up and get the murderous act over.

Terrified by the signed threats coming from their employer, the deaf servants put greater strength into their efforts to kill Mustapha. Eventually, by sheer force of numbers, they were able to throw the prince down and slip the bowstring around his neck and strangle him, to the satisfaction of Sultan Süleyman and Hürrem Sultan.

Shortly afterwards, Mustapha's deformed brother Jehangir also died, and Hürrem Sultan got her wish when Sultan Süleyman decided in 1558 (eight years before his death in 1566) that her son Selim was to succeed him. Outraged, another brother Bayezid rebelled against this decision and engaged Selim in a bloody battle that ended in defeat for him. For this act of rebellion, Hürrem Sultan and Prince Selim had Bayezid and his four sons executed, possibly also by the deaf executioners.

Chapter 2

1769: London, England

The Trial of William Baker

On 23 March 1769, John Palmer, a wigmaker living in Little Duke Street off Grosvenor Square, was at work with his son when Joseph Curtis, a tinman, called in the premises at about 6 p.m.

Curtis was a neighbour from nearby Hart Street and after exchanging gossip, he took his leave of the wigmakers saying he was going to find some grinders to have a pair of scissors seen to. In about 15 minutes, he was back in the wigmakers' shop clutching his left side saying he had been stabbed.

Unbuttoning Curtis' waistcoat and coat, Palmer saw that the other man's shirt and hand were all bloody.

"Who done that?" Palmer asked.

"They were grinders. Two of them. They have done for me", Curtis gasped.

Meanwhile, there had been a commotion nearby as a result of a fracas involving Joseph Curtis. This had started as two brothers were going about their daily business, involving the sharpening and grinding of knives, scissors and the like. Just before Curtis came to have his scissors sharpened, a man who had known one of the brothers in Quebec came upon them and took the brother he knew into a pub called the Running Horse which stood at the corner of Little Duke Street with Oxford Road, leaving the other brother alone out in the street with the grinding barrow, finishing off sharpening. The other brother then came into the Running Horse with the barrow

7

and set it up against a wall in the yard of the public house. It appeared that the crank of the grinder on the barrow was deliberately broken. [*It is more than likely that this had been deliberately broken to aid a practice known as trepanning. In this practice, a trepanner would entrap a person with no means of fending for himself into service with companies such as the East India Company which was heavily involved in Quebec.*]

When the grinder attempted to have it repaired, he was told it would cost one shilling, and the person who had broken the crank objected to the charge, saying he would not pay a farthing and a fracas resulted in which sticks, stones and bricks were thrown against the brothers, one of whom was seen to slap the head of the trepanner twice before they sought refuge in the Running Horse.

According to the testimony of Joseph Wyld given at the trial: "I live and keep a public house in Oxford Road. About seven o'clock that evening, the prisoner and his brother came into my house. There was a great mob at the door. As I went to shut the door, the brother threw something out of his hand into the street. Young Mr. Palmer was there and said, 'Let me in. You know me'. The mob cried, 'There are two men in your house that have stabbed a man. The prisoner and his brother were sat down on a box, and I desired them to walk out peacefully which they refused. The people at the door said they had stabbed Mr. Curtis. Then I opened the door, when three or four of them came in and took them away".

[*Note:-*

In the 17th/18th Centuries many victims of crime were able to identify the culprits and secure their arrest by contacting a constable or justice of the

8

peace. Those who witnessed a felony had a legal obligation to arrest those responsible for the crime, and to notify a constable or justice of the peace if they heard that such a crime had taken place. Moreover, if summoned by a constable to join the "hue and cry", inhabitants were required to join in the pursuit of any escaping felon.

Cries of "stop thief!" or "murder!" from victims often successfully elicited assistance from passers-by in preventing crimes or apprehending suspects, and this is what happened in William Baker's case.]

A London mob at the door of a
public house

Meanwhile, back at John Palmer's house, the mortally wounded John Curtis was helped onto a horse and taken the short distance to his father's house where he was put to bed, and a surgeon named Thompson was called out to examine Curtis.

The two brothers were pushed and jostled along by the mob to the house of a Major Spinnage, who was a justice of the peace, and searched. A small knife was taken out of one of brothers' pockets, but there did not appear to be any blood on them.

The brothers, who were subsequently identified as John and William Baker, were stood before the magistrate as their clothes and possissions were searched. It was observed that the coat and waistcoat that had been brought to the magistrate's attention had two separate cuts, one above the other, on both garments. While they were examining the coat and waistcoat a request came from surgeon Thompson that it was essential Major Spinnage go to the house of John Curtis's father "to take the deposition of the dying man because the wound is mortal, but he was clear of mind at the moment".

[*Note:-*

Before 1829, London did not have a police force in the modern sense of the term. The responsibility for reporting crime, and in large part for identifying the culprits, fell on the victim. Once the accused was arrested, s/he was examined by a magistrate, either in the magistrate's own house or in some other public place. In this case, because of the dying man's injuries, the examination was done in his house. Following the hearing, magistrates were required to commit the accused to prison to await trial, and bind over the victim (and occasionally witnesses) to appear in court to prosecute the case.

Magistrates often tended to dismiss weak cases and only committed the accused to prison if they felt the evidence was sufficent to merit a trial.

Clearly in this case, emotions were running high and it was felt there was sufficient evidence.]

A typical 1750s person who
might form part of a mob or a
press-gang

When Major Spinnage arrived at the house of the
John Curtis' father, the cortege found the dying man
lay on a bedstead, his head turned to the door.

The magistrate instructed the two brothers to stand
at the end of the bed, both handcuffed to each other.

Curtis was asked to point out to those assembled in the room the one who had stabbed him. He took his hand from under the bedclothes and pointed at one of the brothers, "That is the man who stabbed me."

Asked to repeat for the benefit of the record, Curtis again pointed to the one he had previously picked out and said, "Him, with the apron. It was a man with one eye."

The magistrate asked all those present to observe the prisoner indicated, and all agreed that the person pointed out to them had only one eye.

The clerk to Major Spinnage then wrote out a mittimus (a warrant of commitment or command to hold someone in prison signed by a victim and witnessed). This read as follows:

"The information of Joseph Curtis, taken upon oath before me, one of his majesty's Justices of the Peace for the county of Middlesex, the 23rd day of March 1769. John Curtis of Hart Street, Grosvenor Square, now sensible and supposed to be mortally wounded, maketh oath and says, A person now present, who calls himself William Baker, was the very person that stabbed him with a knife on his left side, of which he languisheth and this deponent further says, that another person, who calls himself John Baker, was no way concerned in giving him this wound.

Signed with the – (Mark of) – Joseph Curtis."

William Baker, a man with one eye and also said to be "very deaf" was thus committed to stand trial at the Old Bailey on 5 April 1769 for the murder of Joseph Curtis (who died 3 days after the stabbing).

When the trial took place, evidence and depositions were by all those all those who witnessed (or said they had witnessed) the affray, the arrest and the scene at

John Curtis' deathbed. Particular emphasis was given to Curtis' identification of his assailant.

There was some dispute as to whether Baker had actually stabbed the young John Curtis. The accused denied that he had stabbed the young man, and said there was a lot of jostling going on. He said he took refuge in the Running Horse with his brother when the mob started throwing stones and other things at them.

A witness, Mary Warton, testified that she had seen Mr. Curtis strike the accused (whom she called the grinder) two blows on the head with his hand, but did not hear what the deceased or the grinder said. There was a great mob of both men and boys, she said, and a cry went up about 5 minutes after the original confrontation that Mr. Curtis had been stabbed.

Her testimony was supported by another witness who testified that the deceased had struck the first blow, actually two blows, and the prisoner had moved away. He said that Curtis had gone after him and there were words exchanged in the middle of the road. The witness had thought there was going to be a fight but had not seen anyone use their hands apart from the deceased.

It was clear in court that despite the crowds, on-one had actually witnessed the stabbing of John Curtis.

Two people, Baker's brother-in-law and a woman friend, both acted as character witnesses, saying that they had never known Baker to be involved in a wrangle before. William Baker was always honourable and civil.

Baker was found guilty of manslaughter and sentenced to imprisonment. He was also sentenced to 'branding' – burnt with a hot iron on the thumb (T was for theft, F was for felony and M was for murder). People could only be branded once.

An Old Bailey Branding of the thumb

Chapter 3

1880: New Brunswick, Canada

The Drury Mystery

Like many places on the East Coast of the United States and Canada, the city of St. John's in the province of New Brunswick has a heavy Irish influence. Many thousands of men, women and children trying to escape the Irish Potato Famine of 1845-1852 descended on this small city – at one time, there were more Irish immigrants than there were residents of the city itself.

St. John's Harbour
circa 1880s

Although many Irish immigrants moved on to other places in Canada and the United States, those who stayed on in St. John's contributed much to the development of the city. Indeed, when the centre of St. John's was totally devastated by the Great Fire of 1877, the city was almost entirely rebuilt using Irish labour.

However, not all Irish people who settled in St. John's came because of the Potato Famine. One such person was Captain Charles Vallancy Drury, a soldier in the British 29th Regiment of Foot that was involved in Britain's wars in various parts of North and South America in the early 1800s. He first came to New Brunswick in 1804, when he met and married Frances

Amelia Hazen on 27 December that year. The following year, the couple had their first child, a son named Charles – the only one born in Canada. The following year, Captain Drury was posted back to his home country in County Cork, Ireland, where he had several more children. More postings followed to England, then Wales, then back to Cork before he retired from the Army in 1822 and took his family back to New Brunswick where he took over Newlands Farm, which his wife had inherited from her family. The children that went with the family back to New Brunswick included six sons and two daughters.

Of the sons, John, the second eldest, and Mary, the eldest daughter, were totally deaf, and the youngest brother, Edward O'Brien Drury, was simple minded and hard of hearing.

Only two of Captain Drury's children ever married, Ward Drury who subsequently had four children, and Margaret, who married Sir John C. Allen, the Chief Justice of New Brunswick.

John's elder brother Charles was away serving in the army when his father died in 1836, and John took over the running of the farm on his absent brother's behalf. In 1840, he was charged by an Act of Parliament to spend ten pounds to build and maintain a road (subsequently known as the Great Marsh Road) between the homestead and a hamlet known as Campelltown.

After the return of his elder brother Charles from army service in the 1860s, John continued to assist with the running of the farm. In many ways, it could be said that John was the main person who did the running of the farm – he probably regarded the farm as his own.

Charles Drury died on 21 February 1880, and John got a shock when he found out that the farm had been bequeathed not to him, but to his younger brother, Ward Chipman Drury who moved his wife and his four children into the farm. Although he was allowed to continue living on the farm, as was his simple minded brother Edward (his deaf sister Mary had died in 1867), John no longer had any control over what was happening on the farm. He disliked the changes that Ward implemented on the farm and the two brothers argued frequently over how the farm should be run.

On the night of 2nd June 1880, people living nearby were aroused at 11 o'clock in the night by shouts, screams and gunshots coming from the Drury homestead, and a great orange glow filled the night sky as several of the farm buildings caught fire.

As St. John's new horse-drawn pumpers, pressed into service following the Great Fire of 1877, battled up the hill from the Great Marsh Road to the homestead, curious spectators came from every direction, crowding the lane so that the pump wagons had difficulty getting through, and in any case, the strength of the fire was so strong that the pumps were unable to extinguish the flames, so the buildings burnt down.

Horse-drawn pump wagons, *c*1880

The crowds' excitement was further intensified when two bodies were brought out of the homestead. They were 72 year-old John Drury and his 67 year-old brother, Edward O'Brien Drury. They were also treated to the spectacle of Ward C. Drury receiving treatment for gunshot wounds.

All the other people who had been in the homestead when the fire occurred were unhurt, but distressed. These people included Mrs. Ward C. Drury and her four children, plus three female servants. Two other brothers of John Drury did not live at the farm.

As St. John's police arrived to control the crowds and investigate the fire, they were told a story that saddened all those who knew the Drury family.

It seemed that John had snapped following yet another argument with his brother Ward out in one of the barns, and had attempted to murder him, shooting at him several times but thankfully only hitting him superficially. After setting fire to the barn, John had then gone into the homestead to Edward's bedroom and shot his deaf brother dead as he lay in bed, and set fire to the bed and curtains. When these were well ablaze, John had then retired to his own bedroom and shot himself dead.

The subsequent coroner's verdict found that John Drury, having lost the farm he regarded as his, had murdered his brother Edward and attempted the murder of his other brother Ward, and committed suicide whilst the balance of his mind was disturbed.

Chapter 4

1975: Birmingham, England

Freed into the Community to Kill Again!

When Brian Middleton failed to connect with his daily telephone call to his 83-year-old mother who lived on the tenth floor of a block of flats called Birchfield Tower in Perry Barr, Birmingham, he became concerned. The daily telephone ritual was a means of keeping a check on his mother and satisfying himself she was well, so he called his wife and both of them went to Birchfield Tower fearing that they would find their mother had collapsed.

What they found when they let themselves into the tenth floor flat on 22 April 1994 was much worse than they had feared. Their mother, Rosella Middleton, lay in the living room floor in a pool of blood. She had been savagely battered about the head.

Birchfield Tower

The murder of the elderly, church-loving sparked a wide police manhunt. Inside the murder flat, police found a scarf that neither son nor daughter recognised and it was bagged for forensic examination. Door to door enquiries inside the tower block drew a blank, which was not surprising as neighbours tended to keep to themselves. Despite security measures, it was not unknown for strangers to roam the corridors having got in by devious means.

Rosella Middleton regularly went to church and loved to travel around Birmingham on the buses. She had been last seen at 10 p.m. in John Menzies newsagents shop in New Street station where she had gone, as she frequently did, to buy her evening newspaper and had been caught on the station's CCTV at 10.10 p. m. walking towards the exit. The CCTV did not show anyone else with her or behaving suspiciously.

Rosella Middleton

The brutal murder of an old lady led to rewards totalling £10,150 to be offered for information that would lead to the arrest and conviction of her killer but despite this and intense police enquiries in the locality, there were still no arrests by the end of May.

Meanwhile, police were also involved in another ongoing investigation into a murder that happened less than 6 weeks previous to the murder of Rosella Middleton.

At 7 a.m. on the morning of Thursday 10 March 1994, a butcher arriving for work via the rear of a row of shops on Warwick Road, Acocks Green,

Birmingham discovered the body of a man slumped against trash bins outside a greengrocers.

When the first police officers arrived, they suspected foul play and cordoned off the crime scene to preserve forensic evidence and await the arrival of Home Office pathologist Dr. Peter Acland, who subsequently performed a post-mortem that afternoon.

The man had distinctive features and these were released by police in an appeal to identify the victim. He was fully bearded, had a sleeper earring in one ear and an eagle tattoo on his right forearm. Police also described him as in his 50s or 60s, 5 foot 9 inches tall and scruffily dressed.

He was easily identified as 57-year-old Peter Armstrong, well-known in the locality as Peter the Rabbi due to his full beard and variety of hats that he wore. He frequented a number of pubs around Acocks Green although he lived a mile away in Liddon Road. It was established that he had been last seen the previous night at 9.20 p.m. when he had left the house of his daughter, Mary Bourbage in Emscote Road, Witton to go home. Police said that although he habitually dressed scruffily, he was not a vagrant.

Detective Chief Inspector Michael Slough told assembled reporters that they were seeking to question passengers that travelled on buses around that time of the night between Witton and Acocks Green. He added that the victim, a father of four, had been punched and kicked to death in a particularly vicious attack.

After numerous enquiries and examination of CCTV footage police came to suspect Frank Rudolph

Moe, a 39 year old black male, who lived with his parents and sister in Erdington. Their suspicions hardened when it was discovered Frank Moe had killed before, in very similar circumstances!

In 1975, Frank Moe, then aged 21, had punched and kicked a vagrant named Walter Nevitt to death at the rear of another shopping arcade in Birmingham and was ordered to be detained indefinitely under the Mental Health Act after a trial at Stafford Crown Court ruled in 1976 that he was unfit to be tried because of his disability. At the time of Peter Armstrong's murder, Moe had only recently been released back into the community after being confined for years in a variety of mental hospitals, including Rampton.

Frank Moe was born in Guyana in 1955 and had received only minimal education before his parents brought him with his sister to England in 1971. They settled in

Stafford Courtroom, 1975

Erdington where they were still living at the time of Peter Armstrong's murder in 1994.

Despite his denials and support given by his family, Frank Moe was placed at the Armstrong murder scene by witnesses and forensic evidence and was sentenced to life imprisonment with a minimum of ten years by Birmingham Crown Court.

The arrest of Frank Moe caused the police to look at his possible involvement in the killing of Rosella Middleton because of the way she had been battered about the head with fists with such force that her cheekbone and nose were broken. As Moe had used his bare hands (as well as his feet) in the killings of Walter Nevitt and Peter Armstrong, he was an obvious suspect for another murder committed using bare hands.

However, he could not be positively linked with Rosella Middleton's murder so when he went to Wakefield Prison in West Yorkshire, he was convicted only of Peter Armstrong's murder. The judges were not going to re-commit him under the Mental Health Act again!

By 1998, there had been tremendous improvements made in DNA profiling and a partial profile from the semen found on Mrs. Middleton's clothing was obtained. This was enough for the police to reopen the Rosella Middleton case, and they submitted the clothing and other DNA samples to the Forensic Science Service (FSS) specialist DNA unit in Birmingham. They mounted an intelligence-led screen using samples from suspects who could not be conclusively eliminated from the investigation.

All those screened were eliminated – except Frank Moe. The following year a full DNA profile was obtained by the specialist DNA unit and this again matched Moe. The unit carried out further mitochondrial tests on the hairs found at the scene and again, the result matched.

Opening the case at Birmingham Crown Court, Stephen Linehan, QC, said evidence left on the pensioner's clothing was re-tested following advances in DNA profiling. He claimed tests showed it was from Moe who denies doing the murder.

Linehan told the jury: "At that time in 1994, science had not developed the very accurate tests which are now available. The investigators looking into her murder did not at the time find her killer, but science moved on and new tests were developed." Mr Linehan said the chances of the samples not matching the defendant's DNA profile were one in a thousand million.

Frank Rudolph Moe

The court heard that Mrs Middleton, a mother of two, choked on her own blood as she lay fatally injured in her living room floor. It was claimed Moe battered the widow to death after she had rejected his sexual advances.

"She was rendered unconscious by heavy blows to the head and face. She had bled profusely from her injuries and, unable to clear her airways, choked on her own blood," the court was told.

The court was told that a scarf found at the scene was identical to one Moe owned and contained hairs which came from him. Animal hairs were also found on the item of clothing and it was stated they came from a dog which was owned by neighbours of Moe, who sometimes played with it.

A search of his flat in Erdington also uncovered a photocopied map of the area where Mrs Middleton lived and the church she frequented.

It was alleged that Rosella Middleton was followed into her flat by Moe who had got past the security measures by following another tenant into the tower block.

Moe was deemed fit to stand trial despite his communication difficulties. However he was deemed unfit to instruct his defence counsel who were then obliged to challenge all the scientific evidence.

This meant a whole range of scientists gave evidence at Birmingham Crown Court and continuity was heavily challenged. Scientists took part in two *voire dires* – trials within a trial – to get certain vital parts of the scientific findings introduced as evidence.

Details of his violent past came out after a jury took an hour and 20 minutes to find Moe then aged 45, guilty of murdering Mrs Middleton. He was jailed for life, and the judge, Mrs Justice Smith, said she would be writing to the Home Secretary recommending that he spend the rest of his life in prison.

"It must be recognised by anybody who considers your case that you are a very dangerous man indeed," she said. "I say that notwithstanding your pleasant and often smiling demeanour."

The judge added that she agreed with the police view that Moe was a ruthless and indiscriminate killer who pried on vulnerable victims, adding that she could not imagine a time in the foreseeable future when it would be safe to release him.

Chapter 5

1980: Annapolis, Maryland, USA

The Bad-tempered Carpenter

When neighbours in the Smallwood Village area of Waldorf, Maryland, brought to the attention of Charles County police officers the cries for help of a little boy banging on an upstairs window early one evening on 30 November 2001, what they discovered when they entered the house brought to an end a life of crime that had begun 21 years previously.

On 8 February 1980, Annapolis police were called out to the Yankee Yacht Carpentry Shop by employees who reported that the premises had apparently been broken into and vandalised. One employee was hauling his motorcycle out of the adjoining creek into which it had been dumped.

Inside the shop, which in reality was more of a workshop and boatyard where repairs were made to boats and chandlery items were fashioned, police found bloodstains.

Parked in the boatyard was the van used by the business and its employees. Its tyres were slashed and there was a bloodstained carpet roll in the back of the van. Examination of the vehicle log and its odometer slowed that 40 miles had been driven since the last entry was made in the log.

The owner of the boatyard, Clinton Packer Riley, aged 52, had been reported missing since the previous day, February 7, by his wife.

Initially, police looked upon the incident as a piece of wanton vandalism although the disappearance of the owner was very worrying. Despite extensive enquiries, police failed to find any trace of Clint Riley and feared for his safety.

As the investigation proceeded, they found that the shipwright tended to be argumentative with a number of employees. For example, there had been a fierce row in recent days between Riley and the owner of the motorcycle, and Riley had threatened to dismiss him. Riley's wife confirmed that the night before his disappearance, they had been discussing whether to dismiss one of their employees who was proving to be troublesome.

However, despite all the evidence they had uncovered, police were unable to locate the whereabouts of Clint Riley and the case remained dormant until 22 October 1982 when a couple walking their dog in a wooded area near the Eastern Shore area of Annapolis found some skeletal remains.

Using dental records, an autopsy confirmed that the remains were those of Clint Riley. The autopsy also revealed that the victim had been stabbed repeatedly and struck with a heavy object.

Although the finding of the remains and the autopsy refocused police attention on the original disappearance of Clint Riley, they were unable to further their investigation. They had their suspicions but were unable to convert these suspicions into a conviction.

What they did do, however, was cultivate a relationship with the girlfriend of an ex-employee of the boatyard. In a series of apparently casual meetings, detectives warned her of her boyfriend's record for violence and of his convictions for burglary and theft, for which he had spent short periods in prison. They told her that her boyfriend "may have set several fires,

28

may be involved in the Riley case and may have cut up a neighbour's dog." Police also warned her that the boyfriend had also "been in Crownsville for a while."

Crownsville Hospital Center was the Maryland State psychiatric hospital.

The girlfriend refused to believe police claims "because I loved him". However, the seed of mistrust had been planted in her head, and she began to question her lover about his past.

Through a mixture of sign language, verbal communication and written notes over a dinner table, she elicited sufficient information from him to frighten her enough to terminate the relationship. She was also scared by her boyfriend's temper following the termination of the relationship when he committed several traffic violations and was arrested by police in August 1983.

After agonising for a while, the girlfriend decided to give a statement to the police with the result that on 7 September 1983, more than 3½ years following the disappearance of Clint Riley, police announced the arrest of Patrick Colin McCullough for his murder.

Born in Alaska in 1956 to a military family, his deafness was first noticed at the age of three when he was misdiagnosed as mentally retarded (a term frequently used by Americans to say a person was not developing as s/he should be).

When the deafness was more correctly diagnosed, McCullough was educated through the state deaf school system and came to Annapolis in the late 1970s after training as a carpenter.

He obtained a job as a carpenter with Clint Riley's boatyard in 1979, working on the furnishing of yacht interiors, often riding to work on a motorcycle which he left parked in the boatyard whenever he did not want to ride home. This usually happened when he went drinking in Annapolis.

This motorcycle was the subject of frequent arguments between McCullough and his employer. Riley objected to the machine being left on his premises on a regular basis. This culminated in a final heated argument on 7 February when the motorcycle was unceremoniously thrown into the nearby creek by Riley in a fit of temper.

The ex-girlfriend told the police that McCullough had told her Riley had hit him several times before he retaliated and knocked him down. When he realised that Riley was dead, he had put him into the back of the boatyard van and driven round for sometime before going out to the Eastern Shore and dumping the body.

McCullough had driven the van back to the boatyard and vandalised its tyres and other items in the boatyard to make it look like the work of vandals.

When the case came to trial in February 1984 before Circuit Court Judge Raymond Thieme, care was taken to ensure that Patrick McCullough's rights were carefully protected by the court, to avoid any possibility of a mistrial. Three interpreters were used in court, one for the defence, one for the prosecution and the other for the court itself. Both the prosecution interpreter and the court interpreter were instructed not to look at the defence table whenever McCullough was signing to his attorneys through his own interpreter.

The main witness for the prosecution was his ex-girlfriend, who was summoned to give evidence on the second day of the trial. Because of defence objections to her testimony, which centred around the contention that she did not understand sign language sufficiently well enough to understand the full impact of what McCullough was saying to her during that dinner when allegedly told her of his involvement in the murder of his employer, Judge Thieme ordered the jury out of the room and asked the witness to go through parts of her evidence.

The court heard from the defence attorney that the girlfriend's version of the incident that McCullough was alleged to have told her was inconsistent with versions detailed by other expert witnesses. However, McCullough cried when his ex-girlfriend was testifying and made an unintelligible noise to friends sitting behind him in the courtroom and the judge was satisfied that her evidence was valid and crucial to the prosecution's case and refused the defence's motion to suppress the evidence. He ordered that the witness give her evidence the next day before the jury.

The next morning, Patrick McCullough asked to be allowed to make a statement to the court through his interpreter.

Visibly shaken and upset, he told the court, "I feel like I've decided I'm guilty of the man dying," and pleaded guilty to "man death", his term for manslaughter.

Asked by the judge if he understood his plea, McCullough replied that he understood what guilty meant but was confused by the court process. "I feel like it's a gamble with the jury. I am afraid of the jury."

By saying this, McCullough was implying that if he allowed the case to proceed by not changing his plea, there was a strong possibility that he could be found guilty of either first- or second-degree murder. By pleading guilty to manslaughter, he would face a maximum sentence of ten years if the judge accepted the plea.

Man admits guilt in Riley slaying

By EFFIE COTTMAN
Staff Writer

Cullough stopped dating last summer.

Cullough was unable to tell 1 girlfriend the emotions surroundi

Headline in Washington Post newspaper after
Patrick McCullough changed his plea.

The judge did accept the plea, and instructed the jury to bring in a guilty verdict of manslaughter. Sentencing was deferred to 9 April pending reports assessment from a psychiatrist at St. Elizabeth's Hospital. The sentencing was further deferred to 14 May as the assessment had not yet been completed, but on that date, Patrick McCullough was sentenced to a 7-year term for manslaughter.

Part of the sentence required that McCullough underwent mental health counselling with the Mental Health Center for the Deaf and Hearing Impaired of Lanham, Maryland, to be conducted at the Anne Arundel Detention Center.

One month later, Patrick McCullough was charged with a second murder and was back in the familiar surroundings of Anne Arundel County Courthouse!

Detectives investigating the Riley murder had quietly been checking into the background of the likeable and handsome McCullough and found that he was subject to unpredictable outbursts of temper if things did not go his way, and that he had applied for a job as parking attendant with a garage in downtown Annapolis on 17 February 1982.

Detectives found that around the same time that McCullough's job application had been received and filed by the garage, the night manager, John Porter Myer, had been found bludgeoned to death. At the time, the motive had been thought to be robbery because Myer had been providing cover as parking cashier and the takings for that night had been stolen.

They now realised that McCullough had been interviewed by Myer and been refused the job, and in a fit of temper, he had hit the other man and robbed the garage to make it look like a robbery gone wrong.

Anne Arundel Courthouse, Annapolis

In January 1985, after psychiatric reports had been submitted to the court, McCullough entered an Alford plea. This type of plea originated in North Carolina in 1970 in the case of *North Carolina v. Henry C. Alford*, in which Alford, while maintaining his innocence, pleaded guilty to a charge of second-degree murder, thus avoiding the possibility of a death sentence.

McCullough, in using that plea, avoided subjecting the State of Maryland to a lengthy and expensive jury trial and the possibility of a life sentence, maintaining his innocence whilst conceding there might be enough evidence for a conviction.

Circuit Court Judge Bruce C. Williams sentenced him to a ten-year prison term, to run concurrently with his existing 7-year sentence for the Riley killing. This in effect increased his sentence for the first killing to ten years. The judge recommended that McCullough serve his sentence at the Patuxent Institution, a prison for criminals with psychiatric needs. This was because McCullough's time in Anne Arundel Detention Center had proved unbeneficial, with the counselling programme being cancelled due to McCullough's outbursts which meant he had to be kept away from other prisoners.

In early 1992, McCullough was paroled from the two manslaughter charges but within months of release, he had developed a crack cocaine addiction and to feed this addiction, he committed several misdemeanours including burglary and forging cheques, and was arrested in August the same year and sentenced to a five-year prison term, suspended on condition that he entered a long term residential drug and alcohol rehabilitation programme. He was released on probation from this programme in January 1995.

He successfully shunned drugs and alcohol, working six days a week and a group of friends helped him to finance his first car. An Annapolis attorney, Hollie S. Cutler, who had helped to represent him in his first murder trial, was sufficiently impressed with his progress to hire him and do some home improvements around her house.

"He was a poor, unfortunate guy who had met bad circumstances and was trying to improve his life," she was to say later in a statement.

Patrick McCullough, on one of his early court appearances.

Unfortunately for the lawyer, McCullough saw more in the friendship than Cutler did. He became infatuated with her, and began stalking her. He often introduced her to others as his future wife.

In the end, Hollie S, Cutler was forced to go to court and take out a restraining order that prohibited him from going near her, her office or her house. McCullough ignored this order, breaking into her house on 16 October 1996 and rampaging through her house. He was arrested and taken to court, and reminded of the restraining order.

He continued to ignore the restraining order several more times, and on 2 November 1996, he crossed the center line of the road in his car and smashed into Hollie Cutler's car head-on.

For this act, police arrested him, charging him with aggravated assault, stalking and burglary though McCullough eventually pleaded guilty to only burglary and was sentenced to five years probation.

One of the conditions of the probation order was that he should stay away from Hollie Cutler, yet the day he was released from the county jail, he walked straight to Cutler's law offices. The people there saw him coming and locked the door. As McCullough tugged at the locked door, police arrived and arrested him for probation violation, and sentenced to serve the five years in prison.

In the Maryland Correctional Institute, McCullough spent most of his time weightlifting, doing Bible studies and write letters asking for a reduction in his sentence. In one letter to Judge Michael Loney in October 1998, he wrote: "I promise if you give me another chance, I'll never break the law again."

These letters were to no avail. He was not released from prison until March 2001, when he was paroled.

One of the conditions of his parole was that he had to leave Anne Arundel County, although he could work there). He moved to Grasonville in Queen Anne's County and was found a job with Annapolis Carpentry Contractors Limited, who were charged to provide him with transportation to and from his employment.

In April 2001, he was introduced by a co-worker in Annapolis Carpentry to a woman named Randi Lawrence, a 48-year old single mother who worked at the Rosecroft Raceway.

Randi Lawrence also had a history of substance problems, and was attending local Alcoholic Anonymous meetings. She encouraged McCullough to attend them with her, and began to attend sign language classes so that she could communicate with him.

Friends and neighbours thought they were well suited together, and they were often seen around the Smallwood Village neighbourhood together. Randi even recommended McCullough (whose carpentry skills were never in any doubt) to her neighbours for carpentry work.

Smallwood Village

After a seven month courtship, things seemed to be going well between the pair, then in late October 2001, Randi Lawrence sent McCullough a letter breaking off the relationship.

The police have never revealed what was in the letter, but it was enough to send Patrick McCullough over the edge.

He began coming to her house at night, stalking her in the same way that he previously stalked Hollie Cutler. Although Lawrence asked her relatives to drive by her home occasionally to make sure McCullough was not there, she neither complained to the police about him nor sought any restraining order as Cutler had done.

So when the police broke in to the house in Ferrell Court, Waldorf just after 8 p.m. on the evening of 30 November in response to neighbours' concerns about the crying little boy in the upstairs window, they found that Patrick McCullough had committed his third murder.

He had shot Randi Lawrence with a stolen shotgun, and as her 7-year old son cried upstairs unheard by him, turned the gun upon himself and shot himself, thus bringing to an end a 20-plus career in crime.

Chapter 6

1981: Missouri, USA

The Killing of a Protector

During the summer of 1981, three young deaf men moved into an apartment complex in St. Louis, Missouri, owned by Paraquad, Inc., a non-profit state programme that provided independent housing and a range of other services for disabled people in St. Louis, including vocational training programmes.

The apartment complex was known as Boulevard Apartments and was located at 4545 Forest Park Boulevard, St. Louis. Two young black males, Wallace Spivey and Ronnie Randolph, moved in to share apartment no. 011. A white male, Greg Eisenberg, was given his own apartment, no. 307.

Although all 3 had known each other and socialised in the same circles before moving into Boulevard Apartments, and in fact had spent time together at the same school for the deaf, their lives could not have been more different.

Wallace Spivey and Ronnie Randolph came from poor, impoverished families. Randolph was said by his former school teacher at the Missouri School for the Deaf in Fulton, Missouri, to have had a deprived childhood whereas Spivey was constantly in trouble.

Greg Eisenberg, on the other hand, had a loving family. Born in St. Louis, his family relocated to a farm in a rural community to be near the Missouri School for the Deaf. He developed into an accomplished

Two views of the Missouri School for the Deaf,
Fulton, Missouri

outdoor woodsman and an avid fisherman. He adored animals and loved to ride the family's horse bareback at breakneck speeds. Eisenberg finished his education in a mainstream school so that he could integrate into the community.

Far Left:
Wallace Spivey
Left:
Ronnie Randolph

Both photos from the School Year Book

These, then, were the three men that moved into Paraquad's housing complex in the summer of 1981. There were already other Deaf people in Boulevard Apartments and Paraquad employed Deaf people to act as advisers and counsellors. Eisenberg was also to take part in Paraquad's vocational training programme.

To celebrate their moving in to the apartment complex, they held individual parties during the first week of August to which other Deaf people were invited.

Eisenberg's party in room 307 included his new neighbours, Spivey and Randolph plus three other men, all of whom were white. One of these men, Larry Jackson, was to inform the police later that he only drank two bottles of beer and smoked a very small quantity of marihuana before passing out.

He did not believe that he passed out because of the marihuana or beer he knowingly consumed but felt that he had been drugged. He gained consciousness the next morning in a vacant apartment on the first floor of the Boulevard Apartment complex. His body was in a bathtub filled with water and he was still fully clothes, including his shoes. His wallet and money had been stolen from his pants pocket. No one else was in the apartment when he awoke.

Larry Jackson immediately went to Greg Eisenberg's apartment on the third floor and asked him if he knew what had happened. Eisenberg told Jackson that he thought that Wallace Spivey and Ronnie Randolph had drugged him and had taken him to a vacant apartment to rob him. After Jackson changed into dry clothes, he and Eisenberg went to JEVS, located at 1727 Locust, in the City of St. Louis, a counselling service for Deaf people.

At JEVS, Jackson and Eisenberg saw their counsellor, Dottie Wilcox. They told Ms. Wilcox what Wallace Spivey and Ronnie Randolph, two other clients of Ms. Wilcox, had done to Jackson.

Either later that day or sometime shortly thereafter, Larry Jackson went to apartment 011 and confronted Ronnie Randolph and Wallace Spivey with Greg's accusation. They said Eisenberg was lying and denied having drugged, robbed or placed Jackson in a bathtub filled with water.

Around the same time, Spivey and Randolph had their party in their ground floor apartment. In attendance were a white girl named Doni Stith, her boyfriend Dwayne and another Deaf man named Willie. All of them consumed alcohol at the party in moderate quantities. Doni Stith did not feel that

42

Dwayne and Willie had drunk that much that they passed out. Possibly, in view of what had happened to Larry Jackson, the two men had also been drugged by Spivey and Randolph.

When Dwayne and Willie were asleep, Spivey and Randolph, grabbed Doni and pulled off her clothes. She screamed and tried to get away from them but Willie and Dwayne failed to wake up in spite of her scream because both of them were Deaf. Spivey and Randolph threatened her with a knife to keep her from struggling.

The two men then had sexual intercourse with her without her consent. After the rape, two other men finally woke up.

The day after the rape, she told Greg Eisenberg what Spivey and Randolph had done to her and asked that he protect her from them.

On Saturday 8 August, Dottie Wilcox went to the house of Bill Shelton, a Deaf man employed as a vocational counsellor, and saw Ronnie Randolph there.

Ms. Wilcox confronted Randolph with Greg and Larry Jackson's allegations about the robbery. Randolph admitted that he and Wallace Spivey had stolen Jackson's money but stated that they had already worked it out with him and that everything was settled. Wilcox also told Randolph that she knew about the alleged rape of Doni Stith. He replied that he and Spivey had in fact had intercourse with Doni Stith but that it had been with her consent.

A few days prior to 24 August 1981, she again saw Ronnie Randolph. This time he was with Wallace Spivey and the three of them had a conversation about

Greg Eisenberg. Both Randolph and Spivey told her that they were very angry with Eisenberg. Spivey said that he knew Greg had been gossiping about the two of them in the deaf community. They told her that they knew Greg was telling everyone that they had raped Doni Stith and robbed Larry Jackson.

Greg Eisenberg

On 24 August 1981, Eisenberg told Bill Shelton that he was afraid of Ronnie Randolph and Wallace Spivey because of the threats they had made to him. Later that evening, he had another small party in his apartment with a few friends. Sometime during the evening, Randolph and Spivey turned up at the party, apparently admitted into the apartment by another guest who did not realise the tension between

44

Eisenberg and the other two, who were the odd ones out at the party because they were black and everyone else was white.

Randolph and Spivey hung around until everyone else had gone then confronted Eisenberg. This led to a fight in which Eisenberg was stabbed in the back with a butcher knife which broke, but incapacitated him enough to enable Spivey to strangle Eisenberg from behind, whilst Randolph held down his legs.

Spivey and Randolph then took Eisenberg's watch, wallet and a knapsack before placing the body in the bathtub which was filled with water. The two killers then left the apartment, locking the door behind them.

Greg Eisenberg's body was not discovered for six days, when his father and brother on a pre-arranged visit to his apartment could not get into it. Worried, they called upon the building's janitor to open up and let them in only to be met with a stench that forced them to cover their noses.

The discovery of Greg Eisenberg's murder spread quickly around the Deaf community in St. Louis and came to Dottie Wilcox's notice and she placed a telephone call the same day the body was found to a police officer named Griffin. In her telephone call, Wilcox told the police that she had seen Spivey at a restaurant on earlier that day wearing the victim's wristwatch, which he claimed he purchased from the victim. She also said she had seen Spivey on 26 August with two knapsacks which he claimed he had purchased from the victim. Wilcox knew that Eisenberg himself recently had purchased one of the knapsacks. Wilcox told Officer Griffin that it seemed unusual that the murdered man would sell Spivey his wristwatch because it was a gift from his father. Wilcox also said that the alleged knapsack sale was unusual because Eisenberg told her he bought the knapsack especially for a trip, and was excited about the trip and looking forward to it.

Wilcox told Officer Griffin about an incident in which Larry Jackson had been at a party with Spivey and Randolph at the victim's apartment after which Jackson found himself in a bathtub of water the next morning, with an amount of money missing.

Officer Griffin interviewed Jackson with the assistance of an interpreter. Jackson told Griffin that he had found himself in a bathtub in an apartment on the first floor of the victim's apartment building after a party one evening and that he and the victim suspected appellant and Randolph had been involved. Griffin noted that the victim had also been discovered in a bathtub full of water.

Based on the information from Wilcox and Jackson, Officer Griffin went to Spivey's apartment on 8 September 1981 to interview him and his roommate Randolph. Randolph was at the apartment, but Spivey was at work. Officer Griffin decided interview both men at the same time, so he dispatched two detectives to Spivey's place of employment. The two detectives went there, identified themselves to Spivey displaying their homicide division badges and wrote a note saying "would you come with us, someone wants to talk with you at homicide". Spivey complied with the officers' request and went with them to the police station.

At the police station, an interpreter communicated to Spivey his *Miranda* rights.

During the police interview, Spivey said that a policeman had shown him a black and white photograph of the victim. Spivey then described in detail what the photograph depicted. But in fact, no police photographs were in black and white, and none of them depicted the details Spivey used to describe the picture.

After a lunch break, Randolph was notified that he was under arrest. He became excited and stated that he did not kill the victim, but that Spivey had strangled the victim with a rope. Next Spivey was placed under arrest for the murder. Griffin told him that Randolph had made a statement telling the police what had happened in the apartment. Spivey then made a statement to the police, describing how he killed the victim. In the two men's apartment, police officers found the contents of Greg Eisenberg's wallet.

After their arrests, Wallace Spivey and Ronnie Randolph confessed to killing Greg Eisenberg. They also confessed to having robbed him. Their statements indicated that prior to going to Greg's apartment, Spivey and Randolph discussed killing Eisenberg and that they planned the murder.

It took over two years to bring the case to trail. Both men were tried separately. Randolph was tried first and received a sentence of 99 years to life.

Wallace Spivey, whose lawyers had fought a tough rearguard action disputing evidence and also requesting competency hearings, was found guilty by the jury on 9 September 1983 of capital murder of

Greg Eisenberg. They rejected his plea of not guilty by reason of a mental disease or diminished responsibility.

Judge Richard J. Mehan sentenced him to life imprisonment with the order that 50 years to be served before parole could be considered.

The Old Courthouse, St. Louis
where Ronnie Randolph & Wallace Spivey
were sentenced to life imprisonment.

Chapter 7

1985: Nebraska, USA

"God has forgiven me."

Gayle Dodd and Karen Wells were manning the service desk with another police employee in the 233 South 10th Street police station at Lincoln, Nebraska, at about 6.30 a.m. the morning of Tuesday 23 April 1985 when they noticed a young man enter the building carrying a bundle in his arms. They saw him pause at the entrance and scribble something on a piece of paper, then approach the desk.

Both women noticed that he had a roughly bandaged hand and dripped a trail of blood across the carpet as he approached them.

They noticed that the "bundle" was in fact a baby boy, which the man thrust into the arms of Dodd whilst handing the note, which was by now also bloodstained, to police officer Wells.

The note said that the police should go to addresses at 3501 N.W. Nutwood Court and 2284 Sheldon Street, Lincoln where they would find two dead people.

Whilst patrol cars were despatched to both addresses to investigate, other police officers took the young man and the baby to Lincoln General Hospital in separate cars for treatment and check ups.

Soon, the investigating officers radioed back to headquarters to report a dead body in each location. They were instructed to leave after securing each crime scene whilst search warrants were being obtained from

County Judge Gale Pokorny. These warrants were not issued for five hours.

Meanwhile, it was ascertained that the young man was deaf and a police officer who knew American Sign Language communicated with him briefly. As a result of this brief communication, the young man was placed under arrest and brought back to the police station at 233 S.10th Street. There, the young man identified a white 1973 Chevy Blazer as the vehicle in which he had driven to the police station.

The police station at
233 South 10th Street, the scene of
an early morning drama.

When the search warrants were finally carried out, police entered a trailer home at Nutwood Court, and discovered the body of a woman in her forties slumped in an empty playpen. It appeared that she had fought for her life as she was being stabbed. She was identified as Lucille Curtright, aged 42.

At the Sheldon Street address, homicide investigators found the body of a young woman dead in bed. She did not seem to have known what was about to happen to her. She was identified as Pamela Curtright, the daughter of the other dead woman.

Lancaster County Attorney Mike Heavican told a press conference late on Wednesday 24 April that they had charged James Curtright, aged 20, with the murders of his mother, Lucille aged 42, and his sister, Pamela, aged 22. The baby he had dumped at the police station was Brett Curtright, aged 1, the son of Pamela Curtright.

Both Lucille Curtright and Pamela Curtright were topless dancers at a cocktail lounge/night club called The Night Before in downtown Lincoln.

Lucille (or Lucy as she preferred to be known), was a widow for many years and had been an erotic dancer in Kansas before moving to Nebraska. In an interview given to a newspaper in February 1985, she said that she had been an erotic dancer for nearly 20 years in order to support her son through his schooling at the Kansas State School for the Deaf.

Pamela had joined the US Marine Corps as a teenager and served for several years until she became pregnant by another serviceman. On leaving the Marines, she went to live with her mother who had by that time moved to Nebraska. However, her mother's mobile home was too small for them both, and she moved out to her own rented home.

James Curtright had been brought up by his maternal grandparents in Kansas City for most of his life and had little contact with his mother. When he moved to Lincoln, he lived at first with his mother but they did not get on, so he moved in with his sister. As Pamela could not afford to pay for the upkeep of James as well as the baby, she left it with her mother who became its full-time carer, arranging babysitters whenever she had to work.

The February newspaper article was the catalyst in the lives of all three Curtrights. It was widely read by many people in Lincoln. These included Deaf people, who began to taunt James that his mother was a whore, a slapper and a stripper who flaunted her body for all to see.

Prior to all this, James Curtright did not have a clue what his mother did for a living, and one night three weeks prior to the murders, he went along to The Night Before Lounge and watched his mother in action for the first time.

"He just sat there and drank a 7-up," the manageress of the cocktail bar said. "He'd glance up there while she did her stuff and she'd smile at him." She added that when Lucy's stint ended at 7 p.m., he got up and left the premises without a word.

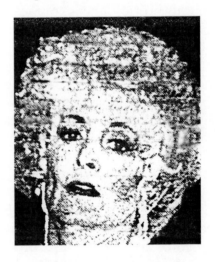

Lucille Curtright

However, Lucy admitted to neighbours Dave Greenlee and Bridget Davidson, who often babysat Brett for Lucy, that her son had not liked what he had seen that night. She said that he felt humiliated that it was his mother doing the topless dance and thought the whole thing had been disgusting.

Lucy told the neighbours that he had gone to his sister's house immediately after the floor show and had told her how disgusted he had been with his mother. He had been totally shocked when Pamela had said to him, "So what? I work there too."

To find out that his sister, whom he had put up on a pedestal although he had rarely seen her during his childhood, was also a topless dancer at the cocktail lounge upset him a great deal. He also did not like the fact that his sister was also sleeping with a succession of men.

"I needed the money," she had told him, "because I wasn't getting any from you!"

James Curtright's financial problems and the new problems he had to confront regarding the profession of his mother and sister caused him to become psychotic with the result that he snapped on that fateful morning, stabbing his sister as she lay asleep in bed.

Then, he got into her Chevy Blazer and stormed off to his mother's mobile home. Dave Greenlee, preparing to go to work, heard a vehicle with a "high acceleration" come down the block.

"I expected to hear it go over the speed bump, but I didn't so I looked out of the window," he said.

He saw a Chevy Blazer, which he recognised as belonging to Pamela Curtright, screech to an halt across the street, a man jump out, then run across the lawn to the door of Lucy's mobile home.

"He got up onto the porch and was banging on the door. I noticed his hand was wrapped in something white and he wore a white shirt and white pants. He stopped banging and tried to open the door but it was locked."

A few minutes later, when he looked again after shaving, he saw the man run out of the house, get back into the Blazer and drive off at high speed. His partner thought the man Greenlee saw and described fitted James Curtright, and told the police this when they turned up at the trailer home about an hour later as a result of information given at the police station.

When the case came to trial in May 1986, a year later, the defence alleged that Curtright was insane during the slayings, but this was refuted by the prosecution who stated that James Curtright's actions subsequent to the killings showed how calm he was. Attorney Heavican said that "he was in control of his emotions and he knew what he was doing. There was no ranting and raving." However, Public Defender Michael Gooch stated the fact Curtright was calm was evidence something was not quite right with him.

"Here's a kid who shows up at a police station, his hands are cut to ribbons, he's just stabbed two people 50 times each and he's as calm as he could be as he delivers a baby to the police."

During the trial, Curtright tried several times to establish eye contact with his grandmother while she testified against him, but she refused to look at him. He also tried to establish eye contact with his grandfather as he sat in court, but the grandfather also refused to look at him.

"I wanted to tell them I was sorry, I didn't mean it," he said.

The jury at the Lancaster County District Court took seven hours to find James Curtright guilty of two counts each of first-degree murder and using a weapon to commit a felony. He did not deny to the court he had killed his mother and his sister, but claimed he was not responsible by reason of insanity.

The Judicial Building, housing the
Lancaster County District Courthouse where
James Curtright had his trial

Curtright said in an interview conducted through an interpreter at the Diagnostic and Evaluation Center where he was being held prior to sentencing that he had found God in May 1986, a few weeks after the killings, and that God had forgiven him.

"But you can't accept punishment just because you've been forgiven," he said. He said he had long supported the death penalty for all murders, and believed that he should be given that penalty.

"I just look forward to meeting God," he said.

After being sentenced to life imprisonment on 3 July 1986, he refused his defence attorneys leave to appeal the decision.

This was despite the warning of his counsel that if he waived the right of appeal, he might lose the right to make a post-conviction appeal under Nebraska law.

But Curtright through a court interpreter told his trial counsel that (translated from ASL):

"I am not willing to appeal. I am guilty. I was wrong. I refuse to allow you to appeal the case. I will not sign an affidavit of poverty or in any other way to do this."

In April 1999, however, Curtright filed a motion for post-conviction relief, alleging that his attorney performed deficiently in not making an appeal, plus amongst other things, having admitted into the trial evidence obtained before his *Miranda Rights* had been read to him. (This was the occasion when the police officer using ASL briefly communicated with Curtright at the hospital, the communication leading to his arrest.)

The State of Nebraska Court of Appeal rejected the appeal on the grounds that Curtright was proved to have expressly, both through a sign language interpreter and in writing, refused his attorney leave to appeal, therefore under Nebraska law, he had lost the right to appeal.

Chapter 8

1990: Montgomery, Texas, USA

Texecuted!

When Linda Purnhagen gave her 16-year-old daughter Gracie money on Wednesday 13 June 1990 to have dinner and go to see a movie together with the youngest daughter, 9-year-old Tiffany, she felt pretty safe in the knowledge that Gracie was a responsible girl who had a 11 p.m. curfew, and would be unlikely to be late given that she had her baby sister with her. Also, the movie was only a short distance from their Oak Ridge North home. She had no idea that Gracie had become involved in an on-and-off relationship with a boyfriend from a dysfunctional family. At the moment, the relationship was "off" but the boyfriend, Delton Dowthitt, who was also aged 16, had unknown to the mother arranged to meet Gracie at the Oak Ridge Bowling Alley to discuss the relationship.

When the rest of the Purnhagen family arrived back home from a auto racetrack event at 2 a.m., they were really concerned to find that neither Gracie or Tiffany were at home, and immediately informed the police.

The Purnhagens became even more concerned when friends of the girls told the police that they had seen Gracie and Tiffany in the parking lot of the bowling alley at 8.45 p.m. talking to two men in a white pickup truck that had a blue stripe across it. At that time, the two girls should have been at the movie.

Gracie was described as 5-foot-5 inches tall, weighing 110 pounds, whilst Tiffany was 4-foot-8 and weighed 60 pounds.

Police enquiries soon established that the two men were most likely Delton Dowthitt and his father Dennis, who suffered from severe deafness as well as mental health problems. They were seen having drinks in the bowling alley's snack bar.

Left, Gracie Purnhagen and right, her sister Tiffany.

Two days later, Deputy Sheriff Mike Worley's attention was caught by the erratic movements of a dusty station wagon along Rayford Road, Conroe, Texas, so he stopped it. It turned out the car had a flat tyre and the driver was trying to drive to a place off the road so that he could leave his car and summon assistance to change the tyre. The car itself was not carrying a spare tyre.

Checking the station wagon's licence, the deputy found that the driver, Ben Fulton, aged 20, was wanted on outstanding traffic warrants. Fulton was taken into custody and transported to the county jail where he was booked in on the warrants. The station wagon was towed to a police compound. Fulton had a passenger in his car, who gave his name as 16-year-old Delton Dowthitt, a workmate of Fulton. At the police compound, Dowthitt telephoned a family member and requested someone came and picked him up. The deputy had been unaware that Oak Ridge North police wanted to question the teenager in connection with the disappearance of the Purnhagen sisters.

Shortly after his arrest, Fulton was bailed by his employer, who then phoned the police the next day to say that another of his young workers had told him he was scared because he had knowledge of a murder.

"He's at my house now and wants to talk to an officer," the boy's boss told police.

Deputy Heather Drennan went to the home, where Pete Brown, a teenage construction worker, told her his colleague Ben Fulton knew about the killing of two girls. Dowthitt was said to have bragged about raping and killing one of them. Fulton had taken him (Brown) to an area near a pipeline and had pointed out two bodies in the brushwood. Brown took Deputy Drennan to the spot and showed her the bodies. They were badly decomposed but were identified as Gracie and Tiffany Purnhagen.

Police were unable to tell immediately how or when the girls had died, or even, whether they had been sexually assaulted because of the decomposition.

Questioned further, Brown told police Fulton had told him that when he was stopped by police, he and Dowthitt were on their way to pick up the bodies, tie them up with cinder blocks and dump them in a creek.

The cinderblocks and rope found in Fulton's car, which were intended to weigh down the two girls after they had been thrown into a creek.

Earlier that day, Dennis and Delton Dowthitt had left for Louisiana with other family members to visit

Dennis Dowthitt's aunt, and it was to New Orleans that sheriff's officers went the next day to enlist the aid of local police in arresting Delton Dowthitt.

At the same time, sheriff's deputies also arrested a friend of Delton named Richard Schuschu outside a motel near Oak Ridge. He was charged with capital murder and aggravated assault. Because Delton Dowthitt was a juvenile, he could not be charged with capital murder but he was nonetheless held in custody for the killings.

A later post mortem conducted on the girls' bodies found that Gracie Purnhagen had her throat slashed and had been sexually assaulted 'with a large rounded object' which had been forced up her back passage. The cause of her death could not be immediately established although her throat was cut and she had been stabbed. Her sister Tiffany Purnhagen had been strangled with a rope. Gracie's body showed evidence that she had still been alive when the assault occurred.

At this stage, police were taking a fresh look at the father, Dennis Dowthitt, who had a previous record for sexual assault. He had access to a white truck with a blue stripe, and on the evening of the 13th June, two witnesses (who were sisters going out with Delton's two older sons) saw the elder Dowthitt in his used car business in Humble and noticed his shirt had blood on it.

Delton Dowthitt had originally confessed to killing both girls. Later, he recanted, saying that he had killed Tiffany on his father's orders. He led police to the spot where the knife was hidden. Police officers later found a bloody bottle with Gracie Purnhagen's blood and

61

Dennis Dowthitt's fingerprint on it in the father's used car business. Also found was the rope used to strangle Tiffany.

Dennis Dowthitt was then arrested and charged with capital murder of Gracie and Tiffany Purnhagen.

Dennis Dowthitt at the time of his arrest

Delton told police his father agreed to drive Gracie and Tiffany home. Instead, his father drove them all in his truck to a remote wooded area in south Montgomery County. There, Gracie and Delton went round the back of the truck to talk privately about their relationship, leaving his father alone in the cab with Tiffany As he and "Gracie" were kissing and making out in the bed of the pickup, suddenly there were screams and cries from the cab and Tiffany ran round to join her sister at the rear of the truck. She was terrified, and he saw his father holding a knife. Saying he had made a mistake, his father told him, "Man, we've got to kill them". He threw Gracie to the ground and slashed her throat, then attempted to rape her. He yelled twice at Delton, "do it", meaning he wanted him to kill Tiffany. He tried to strangle her with his hands, then tied a rope around her neck to finish her off. Delton testified that his father was unable to rape Gracie, so he sexually assaulted her with a beer bottle and ordered him (Delton) to rape her, but he refused. His father then cut Gracie's throat again, and gave Delton the knife, telling him to cut Tiffany's throat. He refused and pocketed the knife.

Both Dowthitts then carried the girls into the woods where the decomposing bodies were subsequently found 3 days later by a pipeline.

Acquaintances of Delton Dowthitt said that he had a history of juvenile offences including at least one allegation of sexual assault. He had dropped out of high school. They did not have anything good to say about him. He was variously described as "an outlaw" and a "very bad kid".

"I don't even want to discuss him. He's very bad news," said a former boyfriend of Gracie Purnhagen, who went on to say that Dowthitt was very possessive and controlling of his girlfriends, subject to violent rages.

Delton Dowthitt

Gracie Purnhagen's older sister, Stacy, told reporters that she had warned Gracie about her relationship with Dowthitt. He had, she said, a lot of tattoos on his arms and was saying things that did not make sense, as if he was doped up.

Because of Delton Dowthitt's testimony, Richard Schuschu was released from custody. He was apparently supposed to dispose of the bodies more thoroughly but the state of the decomposition put him off.

Name: Dennis Thurl Dowthitt   D.R. # 999047

DOB: 6 / 20 / 45   Received: 10 / 30 / 92   Age: 47 (when rec'd)

County: Montgomery   Date of offense: 6 / 13 / 90

Age at time of offense: 44   Race: white   Height: 5-10

Weight: 155   Eyes: green   Hair: brown

Native County: Harris   State: Texas

Prior Occupation: auto sales   Education level: 10 yrs. (GED)

Prior prison record:
None

Summary: Convicted in connection with the deaths of sisters Grace Purnhagen, 16, and Tiffany Purnhagen, 9, in south Montgomery County. The bodies of the two girls were found along a pipeline in the Imperial Oaks subdivision on Rayford Road. Grace's throat had been slashed and she had been sexually assaulted with an object later found to have been a beer bottle. Tiffany had been strangled with a rope found around her neck. Grace's former boyfriend, Delton Dowthitt, then age 16, confessed to killing both girls following his arrest in Louisiana four days later. He later recanted, saying he killed Tiffany at the order of his father, who he said had actually killed and sexually assaulted Grace. Delton led police to where his father had disposed of the knife. Police also found a bloody bottle and rope at Dowthitt's auto sales business in Humble.

Co-Defendants: Delton Dowthitt W/M, DOB: 7/24/73. Reportedly convicted of murder and sentenced to 45 years.

Race of Victim(s): Two white females

Dennis Dowthitt's rap sheet

65

Dennis Dowthitt first went to trial in April 1992, but this was declared a mistrial after three weeks when new evidence came to light. The second trial commenced on Monday 28 September 1992 in Conroe.

At his trial, two of his daughters, Donna and Darla, testified regarding the father's behaviour with them. Donna testified that when she was four or five year old, her father had touched her inappropriately and that when she was 15, he touched her again and asked if she remembered what had happened when she was a little girl. When this later event occurred, Donna left immediately and never lived with her father again.

Dennis Dowthitt's 18-year-old daughter, Darla, told the court that her father was impotent and stated that she went camping with him on the Sunday before the murders. When they were alone, Dowthitt proceeded to threaten her with a knife and sexually assaulted her. She added that Dowthitt had been raping her since she was 11 using bottles and a broomstick on her. Her father had also offered to buy her a car if she would find him a young girlfriend.

Dennis Dowthitt was sentenced to death for his part in the murders. He consistently denied that he was responsible for the deaths of Gracie and Tiffany Purnhagen, pulling all the blame on his son Delton. There were some grounds for believing this to be true because a police report (which the jury did not see) indicated that Delton Dowthitt had previously taken a former girlfriend to the same place where the bodies were found. He had called this road 'rape road'. When this girl refused to have sex with him, he had strangled her into unconsciousness. He had then raped the unconscious girl who did not report the rape until after Delton's arrest.

Also, Delton had bragged of the murders to several friends before he was arrested and had continued to do so since his father received his death sentence. He also had the murdered sisters' names tattooed like a trophy on his body.

However, on 7 March 2001, just before he was executed by lethal injection, Dennis Dowthitt made a last statement to the victims' family behind the glass screen:

> I am so sorry for what y'all had to go through. I am so sorry for what all of you had to go through. I can't imagine losing two children. If I was y'all, I would have killed me. You know? I am really so sorry about it, I really am.
>
> I got to go to sister, I love you. Y'all take care and God bless you.
>
> Gracie was beautiful and Tiffany was beautiful. You had some lovely girls and I am sorry. I don't know what to say.
>
> All right, Warden, let's do it.

His apology finished, the lethal injection was administered and he was pronounced dead at 6.18p.m.

Dennis Dowthitt was the 5th murderer executed in Texas in 2001, and the 244th since the death penalty was restored in 1982.

In exchange for testifying against his father, Delton Dowthitt pled guilty to murdering Tiffany Purnhagen and was sentenced to 45 years in prison. In 1996, he was caught attempting to escape and received another 6 years. He became eligible for parole in 2005 but was still in prison at the time of writing (April 2006).

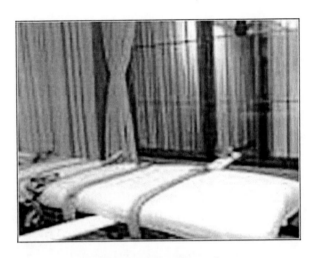

The death chamber where
Dennis Dowthitt was executed.

Chapter 9

1993: Florida, USA

The Man who had a Wad of Money

When 16-year-old Beth Teas spotted a man entering the back entry of the house next door and afterwards drive off in their car, she knew something was wrong. Although she had previously seen the man occasionally visiting the people who lived there and mowing their lawn, she knew that her elderly neighbours, a Deaf couple, were very unlikely to allow their prized car to be driven by anyone else, so she called the police.

When Sheriff's officers arrived a few minutes later on Friday 19 February 1993, they found that the back door had been forced. Inside, they found Betty Gray, aged 60, dead in her bed and her husband, Matthew, aged 63, critically injured in the lounge. The house was also ransacked and they found no money in either Betty Gray's purse or Matthew Gray's wallet.

The medical examiner was later to testify that Betty Gray had died from numerous head wounds consistent with hammer blows. She had been attacked whilst she was in bed with her head on the pillow, possibly asleep. The attack was so strong that only one defensive wound was found on the victim's left forearm; blood and hair were splattered throughout the room, including the walls and ceiling.

Matthew and Betty Gray were both Deaf, staunch members of the local Pinellas deaf community and there was no doubt the killer had known the couple would not hear the break-in. It was also quite likely Betty Gray had not even known who was attacking her.

Beth Teas' description of the man who had driven away in the Gray's car left no doubt that it was a man named Robert Hawk.

Aged 18 at the time, Hawk had been expelled from school for emotive and behavioural problems. He was regularly drunk or drugged. He was said to consume an average of four pints of beer daily as well as using LSD and/or pot (marijuana) up to fifteen times a day. He lived in the same neighbourhood as Betty and Matthew Gray, and had known the elderly couple since he had been 9-years-old, regularly going around to their house. He had been Deaf since aged 3 when he contacted spinal meningitis which was said to have led to his behaviour problems.

In their search for him, sheriff's deputies came across other members of the local Deaf community who told them that Hawk had been flashing a wad of money – something that he had never been known to do in the past – and bragged of killing someone for their car.

The same group of people also told the police that three days prior to the murder, Hawk had bragged to them: "I can, you know, hit, beat up old people."

When Robert Hawk was known to be back at home, Detective Michael Madden together with a sign language interpreter went to the house and asked if he would come to the police station with them voluntarily. Hawk agreed and at the station, Detective Madden had his Miranda rights read to him through the interpreter.

The interview lasted 40 minutes and was audiotaped and transcribed, but not videotaped. At the end of the interview, Hawk was charged with the murder of Betty Gray and attempted murder Matthew Gray. Later, when the trial took place, the police were criticised for not taking the time to obtain and set up the necessary equipment to videotape his interview with Robert Hawk on the grounds that an independent interpreter could not authenticate the proceedings.

When the trial opened in the cavernous Courtroom A of the 34-year-old courthouse in Clearwater, Florida, on Tuesday 19 March 1996, more than three years after the murder, there were 60 people waiting to be selected for jury service and by the end of the first day, a jury of nine men and three women plus two alternates had been chosen.

The trial was the first time in Pinellas County that a system called speech-to-text (STT) reporting was used in court. This allowed for instantaneous transcript of the trial on a keyboard to a video monitor as it proceeded, so that Hawk could read it if he wished. However, most of the time he preferred to watch the court-appointed sign language interpreters – both of whom came from out of the State of Florida because so many of the witnesses as well as Hawk and one of the victims, Matthew Gray, were users of American Sign Language (ASL), and the court needed to have independent and impartial interpreters who were not known to any of the Deaf people in the trial.

However, the acoustics in Courtroom A were so bad that both the ASL interpreters and STT reporters frequently had to ask for testimony to be repeated.

Pinellas County Courthouse in Clearwater, Fla.,
built in 1962 with a terrible acoustics problem

During the trial, there were defence objections to many of the comments uttered by the prosecutors, particularly in relation to Robert Hawk. At various times, Hawk was referred to as "an amoral, vicious cold-blooded killer", "a vicious killer", "a savage killer." All objections were overruled by judge.

On another occasion, Hawk was referred to as "a high school drop-out, unemployed, living off his parents' couch and out of their refrigerator", when in fact he had been expelled as previously stated and rode a moped to his various casual jobs.

In his own testimony during the trial, Hawk accused the Grays of sexually abusing him while he was a child. This was described as an "outrageous allegation" by the prosecutor and condemned by some members of the Deaf community outside the court as a lie.

"I don't believe that", said a personal friend of the Grays. "Every word he said, he's a liar".

Betty and Matthew Gray were portrayed in court as a decent, retired Deaf couple devoted to each other who enjoyed participating in local deaf community events, particularly visits to bingo halls, and took pride in maintaining their 1991 car.

Robert Hawk, on the other hand, was known as an emotionally disturbed young man and such a pathological liar that many of his friends disbelieved him when he told them he had shot some people. One of his Deaf friends remembered seeing Hawk at the ice and roller skating rink that was owned by Hawk's parents. This was stated to be around the time of the murder and when Hawk said a Deaf couple had been killed in his neighbourhood (and this was before the facts had become known), his friend did not believe him because Hawk was known for "telling stories".

On Saturday 23 March 1993, the jury took only two hours to return verdicts of guilty to the counts of first-degree murder and attempted first-degree murder for killing Betty Gray and wounding her husband, Matthew.

The following week, during the sentencing phase, the prosecutor made the following argument: "Mrs. Gray had wounds to her neck, she had wounds to her forehead, she had wounds to her mouth, evidence that she's trying to move to get away from this hammer".

Defence Attorney: "Objection. Facts not in evidence".

Judge: "Overruled".

"She's struggling as best she can in her nightgown, in her own bed, to get away from attacker. Struggling to somehow defend herself... in a vain attempt to ward off the blows by the vicious killer that you have found guilty of her murder... You can look at the evidence in this case and establish whether or not this was a struggling between a defenceless sixty-year-old woman and a healthy, yet lazy eighteen-year-old man".

At the end of this closing argument, the defence attorney moved for a mistrial because of the prosecutor's inflammatory argument. He argued that the State had introduced no evidence to support the argument. The mistrial request was made before the jury was instructed or released to deliberate, as required by the Court. He was denied a mistrial or curative instruction.

During his penalty phase closing argument, the prosecutor also made a "message to the deaf community" argument. He told the jurors that if they recommended life merely because Hawk was Deaf, "that recommendation is an insult to all who have achieved greatness and lived law abiding and productive lives in spite of the same handicap". The judge again denied a defence request for mistrial and request for curative instruction.

Circuit Judge Charles Cope sentenced Robert T. Hawk to death for the murder of Betty Gray.

His defence attorney immediately appealed, and in a judgement delivered in the Florida Court of Appeal on 17 September 1998, the Court overturned the death sentence citing two mitigatory circumstances, (a) the youth of Robert T. Hawk at the time of the murder; (b) that his capacity to appreciate the criminality of his conduct was substantially impaired at the time.

Robert T. Hawk

The Appeal Court also criticised some of the prosecutor's inflammatory comments and in particular his "message to the deaf community", which was felt to be an appeal to any prejudices the jury might have about D/deaf people.

The Court also pointed out mitigation that the trial judge failed to consider, and which was supported for the record. For example, Hawk wrote a letter to the judge asking forgiveness and for a life sentence. He said he was sorry, wanted to give his life to the victims, was embarrassed and ashamed of his behaviour, and wanted to be a good man. Thus, the trial court should have considered remorse in mitigation. Also, although Hawk's counsel did not request it, the judge, who was required to review the entire record for mitigation, could have considered the lack of significant criminal history mitigator because Hawk had no prior violent felony convictions. In fact, he had very little criminal history. When he was seventeen, he was involved in the burglary of a Winn-Dixie Store with several other boys who left him to take the blame. Hawk only held the plywood boards back while the other boys entered the closed store to steal beer and cigarettes. The following year, Hawk was charged with having sex with a fifteen-year-old deaf student who claimed he was her boyfriend, and apparently had consented to the sex. The conviction was for carnal intercourse with an unmarried person under the age of eighteen – a crime rarely prosecuted.

The appeal was upheld and a life sentence substituted without the possibility of parole for 25 years.

Chapter 10

1996: San Francisco, California

A Tale of Love, Mystery & Determination

They were just two young women, both aged just 19, who fell into prostitution to earn themselves some money, and who just vanished.

There were also two young men who loved these women, who both met by chance, and together, were determined to solve the mystery of their disappearances and try to bring those responsible for the crimes to justice. These young men turned amateur detectives when they were confronted by the indifference of the police to the disappearance of their loved ones.

The first to disappear was Melissa Short. It was Christmas 1996, and she had just finished putting up a large Christmas tree in her home that she shared with her boyfriend Freddie Houston and their daughter Luchiana, who was just nine months old.

Originally from Reno in Nevada, Melissa had a good childhood and was an excellent student up to the age of 13 when she fell in with a disreputable crowd and started dropping out of school. She also periodically ran away from home but when aged 16, she returned to and graduated from high school after the birth of her son, whose custody was subsequently given to Melissa's mother.

At the age of 17, she left Reno and moved to the Bay area of San Francisco where she met Houston, a landscape gardener with a criminal record for assault and drug use. A car accident prevented Houston from working, and it fell to Melissa to earn enough money to rebuild their lives. She did this by becoming a prostitute and working the streets.

Freddie Houston knew that his girlfriend was a prostitute but did not try to stop her. "She was strong-willed and had her own opinion. She did her thing and I didn't try to stop her," he told news reporters later.

At about 11 p.m. on the night of 23 December, she kissed Houston and her daughter goodbye and left home to keep an appointment with a customer that was scheduled for 12.30 a.m.

She never came home and a very concerned Houston went to the Contra Costa County Sheriff's Department to report her missing, but was told that he could not file a missing person's report for 72 hours.

The fact he had a criminal record and was known to the Sheriff's Department did not help.

Houston spent a miserable Christmas, waiting the three days to pass, then went back to the Sheriff's Department and officially reported Melissa Short missing.

Houston also told them of Melissa's last scheduled appointment. He said this was with a man named Dale Holmes, whom Melissa had "serviced" before because she knew a bit of American Sign Language, and Holmes was Deaf. Also, Melissa used a writing board to communicate with Holmes when it proved too difficult to communicate with him in ASL. Houston gave this board to police officers led by Sheriff's Detective Andre Charles, and insisted the officers accompany him to Holmes' home, where he lived with his brother, sister and mother. Despite Houston's pleas, police refused to undertake a search of the Holmes residence, saying they had no justifiable cause to do so and there was no evidence to enable them to seek a search warrant.

Freddie Houston was so angered by police indifference to his missing partner that he himself became the prime suspect in Melissa Short's disappearance.

Despite police indifference, Houston continued to frequent the Tenderloin district of San Francisco asking questions of other girls walking the streets about Melissa.

In the course of these inquiries, he bumped in May 1997 into a man known only as "Joey" because he was married and did not want his wife and family to know about his extra-marital activities.

"Joey" had a girlfriend he was in love with, and she, too, had disappeared around 29 April 1997. The boyfriend also knew that his girlfriend, Shelly Morrow, was a prostitute. Only three weeks before her disappearance, he had paid for her to have breast implant surgery to make her more desirable to her customers.

"Joey" had first known her as a computer programmer when she moved to San Francisco from Monterey County in November 1996.

The two girls knew each other in passing. In fact, like Melissa Short, Shelly Morrow knew a little ASL and she had compared notes with Melissa about Dale Holmes, particularly Holmes' tendency to page

Melissa regularly. "He's driving me crazy," she had told Morrow according to "Joey."

Left: Melissa Short and
Right: Shelly Morrow.

Although Morrow was worried about Melissa Short's disappearance, she continued to see Dale Holmes, who bore a striking resemblance to the actor Tom Sellack. Holmes paid her well, about $500-$600 a time and on one occasion, $1000.

On May 18, two days after Morrow's disappearance had been reported by her flatmate, the two men met up again and went over to the Holmes' residence at about 2 a.m.

It was a dilapidated house on North Rancho Drive in a small town named El Sobrante. Bicycles, scrap metal and broken down cars were strewn in front of the home. This was not surprising, as the brothers earned their living as scrap metal dealers.

They took with them a flyer about Melissa Short. Raymond Holmes, Dale's brother, answered the door and "Joey" shoved the flyer into his face and asked him, "You seen this girl?" However, Raymond

Holmes turned his head away quickly and said, "No," without even looking at it.

Convinced that Raymond Holmes knew something about Short's disappearance, there was a fracas as the two men threatened Holmes and attempted to pull him into their car.

Raymond Holmes fled.

The persistence of the two prostitutes' boyfriends in harassing the Holmes residence led to a new development in the case.

Four days after the threats to Raymond Holmes, an informant called the San Pablo Police Department and said he could link the Holmes brothers to the disappearance of the two women.

On a hot June morning, dozens of Contra Costa Sheriff's deputies got together at the end of the North Rancho Road, where the Holmes brothers had their residence. This was where the road petered out in a field covered in poison oak. There, the badly decomposed nude body of Melissa Short was dug up. Weeks later, the coroner would determine that she had been stabbed 15 times and had died when the knife pierced her heart.

Dale Anthony Holmes, aged 31, and his brother, Raymond Leslie Homes, aged 29, were both arrested at their nearby home.

Following questioning, Raymond Holmes led detectives to a ravine off a long, winding road on the top of a hill west of Crockett, about 7 miles from El Sobrante. The ravine contained debris tipped over from many years of dumping. There, police found the body of Shelly Morrow. Her body was also badly decomposed, and she had been stabbed 6 times and had been dead about a month when her body was recovered.

Although Contra Costa police officials disapproved of the way the two men had threatened Raymond Holmes' life and carried out what they described as an attempted kidnapping, they conceded that their threats were something that had "loosened his lips."

"The two boyfriends really did all the legwork, they cracked the case," a police officer admitted.

Dale Holmes was charged with two counts of murder in the first degree, and Raymond Holmes was charged with assisting with the disposal of the bodies. Bail was refused in the case of Dale, whilst $1 million bail was set in Raymond's case, Judge Harlan Grossman of Contra Costa County Superior Court denying a defence request for bail on the grounds that Raymond Holmes could have prevented the second woman's murder if he had come clean about the first one.

The motive for both killings was apparently arguments over money, like how much Dale Holmes should pay the women for their sexual services.

After several false starts, it was decided that the brothers would be tried separately, and when he appeared in Contra Costa County Superior Court on 11 December 1997, Raymond Holmes pleaded guilty to charges of assisting in the disposal of the two women's bodies and for assisting in the concealment of a capital crime.

He was sentenced to 16 months in the state prison, but was released immediately because of the time he had served whilst awaiting trial.

Contra Costa County Courthouse, Martinez

Dale Holmes in communication with a sign language
interpreter during one of the competency hearings in
court

Dale Holmes continued to be held in custody pending a preliminary hearing. There were questions over his competency to plead and understand the charges.

Whilst he was being examined by mental health experts, Dale Holmes was confined to Patton State Hospital and it was not until 5 March 2001 that he appeared before Judge Mary Ann O'Malley and requested that he withdrew his previous plea of Not Guilty and entered a plea of not guilty by reason of insanity. This was accepted by the court which imposed a maximum sentence of 52 years to Life, with 1408 days credit for time served.

Chapter 11

1998: San Francisco, USA

The Oldest Killer

At 5 o'clock Thursday morning 23 April 1998, Sergeant John Sterling was looking forward to the end of his shift at Taraval police station, San Francisco, so that he could go home and have some sleep when the telephone rang. It was a 911 call, used for emergencies throughout the United States. Picking it up, he heard a man say in a loud voice, "I just killed my wife." Then the line went dead.

The call was traced to a building in Lurline Street in the Sunset District of San Francisco, and a patrol car was immediately dispatched to investigate.

When the first police officers arrived, they found an elderly man lying on the concrete in the back yard, screaming and moaning. He had several broken bones, and it was evident at first glance that the man had jumped from a second storey window.

Upon entering the house, the officers found an elderly woman dead in her bed, with a plastic bag over her head. She had been bludgeoned several times, and it was clear that the barbell that was lying on the floor was the murder weapon.

As the elderly man was being transferred to an ambulance to take him to San Francisco General Hospital, he told police officers, "Her life was horrible. My wife was a diabetic. She just got out of hospital. She urinated every 10 minutes. She couldn't move any more." He said that he and his wife had made a suicide pact, but when she changed her mind, he killed her because he could not cope any more with her illness, and had jumped out of the window to kill himself.

Investigators discovered that the man was Charles Bauld, aged 90, and his wife, Alicia, was aged 86. He was the oldest man ever to be arrested for murder in San Francisco.

San Francisco General Hospital, where Charles Bauld was taken to recover from his injuries and arrested for the murder of his wife.

As Charles Bauld recovered in hospital with a broken elbow, knee and leg, the head of the homicide unit, Lieutenant David Robinson said of the case, "No matter what his age, he committed a murder. He has to have some accountability for his crime, even though it's obvious he was trying to kill her and commit suicide. He didn't show any glee for killing her. There weren't any signs of remorse but he wasn't particularly proud of himself." Robinson added that although there might have been a suicide pact, there were indications from the scene that she had tried to resist being bludgeoned.

Charles Bauld was born in Tasmania, Australia and had gone to sea as a boy of 16, becoming a US citizen in 1937 having worked for many years on American ships. In 1950, after 25 years at sea, he settled in San Francisco where he met Alicia Trujillo, a Colombian immigrant. A year later, they were married but Charles found the lure of the sea too much, and after studying for his Master's certificate, obtained a new posting as a ship's captain. It was not until Charles Bauld lost his hearing completely and retired that the couple really began to live together properly.

As Alicia's health began to fail, with painful arthritis and heart problems, Charles cared for her, often struggling to carry her up and down the stairs. Neighbours said that Charles would baby her, buy her little gifts and take her out to lunch, but he was in no shape to care for her full time.

One night, she fell in the bathroom and broke her hip. She shouted for him for hours, but because of his severe deafness, Charles did not realise anything was wrong until the next morning. "She was on the floor all night," a neighbour said and in extreme pain.

On her return from hospital, Alicia was confined to bed and a doctor told Charles to put her in a nursing home, but he was totally against such places, calling them "hell holes". So, in the last month before Alicia was killed, a nurse came to help out, for four hours a day.

Also, his brother Ronald came over from Australia with his wife to visit.

"I was very disturbed at the situation. Charles was cooking, cleaning, caring for Alicia and doing all the chores whilst his wife was in and out of hospital. I tried to influence him to get help, but he wouldn't have it. He said, 'I'll struggle to the end.'"

When he got back home in Australia a week before she was killed, Alicia telephoned him. "She said she was tired of being sick. She was very ill and wanted to die. She said they were going to commit suicide."

The day he killed Alicia, Charles had told the nurse not to come in, a neighbour told police.

In the period after he killed his wife, Charles Bauld threatened to commit suicide several times, and had to be placed in psychiatric care on anti-depressants.

Although the police and prosecutors took the stance that Charles Bauld, irrespective of his age, had to be treated the same as any other murder defendant, his mental and physical state, as well as his deafness, plus the nature of the offence gave them serious concerns.

"I hope the case never comes to trial," a public defender said. This was echoed by his brother, Ronald, who said in early 1999 that his brother was now very skinny, very weak.

"He is now in a rest home. I'd be really surprised if anybody wanted to push this case through court. I can't imagine taxpayer money being spent on a big trial for him."

Whilst investigating this case in 2002 in San Francisco, the author was told the case "was now closed". Presumably, this meant that Charles Bauld had died without going to trial.

Chapter 12

1999: Kiribati, Oceania

A Family Feud

Mention a Pacific island, and one immediately thinks of peaceful setting consisting of sun, sea, sand, low-lying atolls and friendly natives. There is no doubt that the islets that make up Tarawa in the Republic of Kiribati falls into this category for it is blessed with long beaches of white sand.

However, a closer look will tell you that here and there, you will find rusting hulks and relics of the Battle of Tarawa between the US Marines and the Japanese in November 1943 that preceded the famous Battle of Iwo Jima.

The Republic of Kiribati formerly consisted of the Gilbert & Ellice Islands which gained independence from Britain in the 1970s. Later, the Republic enlarged to take in the Phoenix and Line Islands, some of which were US-administered. The Line Islands include Christmas Island where Britain tested its atomic bombs in the 1950s. Altogether, the Republic now comprises of a total of 33 atolls spread across hundreds of square miles of sea, of which 21 were inhabited supporting a population of just over 96,000.

Tarawa is the capital of Kiribati; with an impressive brand new Parliament building and other official buildings, including the courthouse, on the islet of Betio. These buildings house the Court of Criminal Jurisdiction and Court of Appeal.

The new courthouse held an appeal session in March 2001 that sorely tested the wisdom and patience of the court when the convictions of two brothers were upheld.

The story began many years back with a family feud between the Tabuki clan and the Kautu clan. Ill-feeling continued down the years on the small island where they lived.

One day in 1999, Rotu Kautu and his wife Riaua were out walking up a track from a beach when they met the brothers Temaua and Tiare Tabuki. Both men were armed with knives and metal spears, and it was evident that both men had been lying in wait for the married couple.

Rotu Kautu was too proud to turn and run, and handing over his back-pack to his wife, he stood his ground and prepared to defend himself. He did not have a weapon.

Riaua Kautu ran to a derelict boat that was drawn up on the shore and collected a piece of timber and ran back to give it to her husband to use to defend himself. Unfortunately, the piece of timber was rotten and it broke when he tried to use it to fend off the knives and metal spears being used by the brothers. Seizing their opportunity, they stabbed him and as he fell down and lay wounded on the ground, attacked him further.

Meanwhile, Riaua Kautu was running towards a small village, screaming for help. When the villagers she had called upon to help arrived at the place where the attack had taken place, they found Rotu Kautu beyond help. He was dead from a severe beating and numerous stab wounds.

The Tabuki brothers were soon arrested by the island police and brought before the magistrates court and charged with murder. It became obvious that the prosecution would have severe difficulty pursuing the case through the courts. The reason for this was that Tiare Tabuki was deaf and unable to speak. Also, there was no expert medical evidence of the cause of death. The doctor who had examined the body had left the island and was unable to give evidence.

Furthermore, in common with many other deaf people throughout the Pacific islands, Tiare Tabuki had never received any form of education. There were no sign language interpreters in Kiribati who could assist translation in court. Although the official language in Kiribati was English, most inhabitants spoke or understood the local native language called I-Kiribati.

It was definite that Tiare Tabuki did not understand any form of English, and it was doubtful whether he understood any I-Kiribati either. What he did have were several family members who could communicate with him of a sort in mime and gesture, but the court could not accept these people as official interpreters due to their family connection with the accused.

Eventually, court officials found someone unrelated to the accused who could communicate with him in a basic manner, and through this communication, it was resolved by the Chief Justice that Tiare Tabuki would plead guilty to the manslaughter of Rotu Kautu at arraignment in the criminal court.

Likewise, Temaua Tabuki (who was not deaf and perfectly able to speak in his own defence) was found by the Chief Justice also to be guilty of manslaughter, and he sentenced both brothers to a mere four years imprisonment each.

Tarawa Island, Kiribati

The Attorney General for the Republic of Kiribati was not happy with the verdicts and the sentences imposed by the Chief Justice, and using the Court of Appeal Act, 1980, he sought to overturn the verdict and thereby increase the sentence. He argued that the two brothers were involved in a "joint enterprise", being armed with the intention to do harm to their victim.

"Actions speak louder than words," he told the court. "Here we have two men, both armed, together attacking another man who at first had no weapon with which to defend himself and then only a piece of rotten wood. The assailants kept on attacking until the victim fell down. That is sufficient to convince me beyond reasonable doubt that this was a joint enterprise between the two men."

This, argued the Attorney General, amounted to murder, not manslaughter, therefore the conviction should be overturned and a re-trial ordered. If a new trial was held, and both men were found guilty, they would be subject to a death sentence.

The House of Parliament and Courthouse on Betio Island, Kiribati.

The appeal was heard by three experienced justices who were brought in from Australia and New Zealand to give the court the benefit of their wisdom. It was dismissed on the grounds that the Chief Justice had taken into account and returned a verdict based on the inability of Tiare Tabuki to understand any part of the criminal proceedings.

The manslaughter convictions and sentences were upheld.

Chapter 13

2000: Cairo, Egypt

The Consequences of a Rejection

When Ahmed Ghanem was asked by Ahmed Hegazi for permission to marry his beautiful 16 year-old daughter, Waheeda, he did not hesitate to reject the request. For one thing, Waheeda was still at school, the Cairo School for the Deaf; for another, Ahmed Hegazi was not long out of the school himself and was only 19 years-old. Ahmed Ghanem told Hegazi to go away and make sure he had prospects before he thought about marriage to Waheeda.

That the father could communicate to Hegazi in Egyptian sign language was not surprising because the Cairo Deaf School ran a teach-the-parents sign language project to enable families of deaf children to learn how to communicate with each other. Also, Waheeda was a popular girl and the Ghanem home in the southern Cairo suburb of Dar Al Salam was often full of her deaf friends.

Ahmed Hegazi left the Ghanem residence hurt and resentful over the father's treatment of him and arranged with a group of friends from the school, including Waheeda's best friend, 17 year-old Seham Hassan, to go on a night out in Cairo. Ahmed's aim was to get Waheeda Ghanem alone and talk to her about her father's rejection of his request to marry her.

It was arranged that a girl called Seham Hassan pay a call on her friend and persuade her to go out. Ahmed

Ghanem had known Seham for many years, and had no reservations in letting Waheeda go out with her friend. However, Seham took Waheeda to meet a group of other Deaf school friends. One these (four young men and two girls) was Ahmed Hegazi.

Because they all knew each other from the same school and also the same deaf club (which was actually based in the school), Waheeda had no hesitation in joining them for the evening. Later in the evening, the group wanted to hire a taxi to take them to El Salam City, a north-east Cairo location near the desert. However, Seham Hassan said she did not want to go there as she had to be back home with her parents but Waheeda decided to go with them, and the group went off without Seham.

Cairo traffic is among the world's worst; taxis are regularly used and Waheeda took her last ride in one.

When his daughter did not return home that night, Ahmed Ghanem went to the police and reported her missing. Mr. Ghanem told the police officers assigned to the investigation of the missing girl that she had left his house the previous evening with Seham Hassan.

When the police went to the Cairo School for the Deaf to question Seham, she denied any knowledge of the whereabouts of Waheeda. Indeed, the police came up against a conspiracy of denial and silence from the other pupils of the school. Their inability to understand deaf culture and to communicate in Egyptian sign language did not help to make matters easier, so the investigation ground to an halt.

Three weeks after Waheeda's disappearance, a girl's badly decomposed body was found in the water by a pumping station in the Delta, an area about 50 kilometres north of Cairo. Investigators called in her father who positively identified Waheeda by the clothes she had been wearing when she disappeared.

The medical examiner's autopsy of the body brought to light several puzzling factors. Despite being found in the water, the victim had not drowned; in fact her throat had been slashed and she had been stabbed to death. Moreover, there was evidence that the body had not been thrown in the water immediately after death as there were traces of desert sand in some of her wounds that the canal and river water had not been able to completely wash out. The autopsy showed it had been at least 2-4 days after death before the body had been dumped in the water where it had remained, carried along by the current until it ended up at the pumping station.

As the police unravelled the mystery of Waheeda Ghanem's death, other investigators found a taxi driver who remembered taking a group of young deaf people from the Dar Al Salam suburb in southern Cairo to a point past El Salam City in north-east Cairo where the desert began. The taxi had left the group there.

The police investigation, which was now under the personal direction of General Seif Al Din, the Director of Cairo Security, once again focused on the school, and resulted in the group of six school pals who had travelled with Waheeda being identified, arrested and brought to court.

The police case was that when the group of six arrived at the desert spot, Ahmed Hegazi and Waheeda walked off into the night of the desert, leaving the others behind. Once out of sight of the rest of the group, Hegazi relieved his anger and humiliation of Mr. Ghanem's rejection of his marriage request and brutally raped Waheeda.

After the rape, Hegazi strolled back to the main group leaving Waheeda weeping on the desert sand and told them what he had done. Some of the group disapproved and told Hegazi that the girl was sure to tell her father what had happened and that he (Hegazi) would be arrested for rape. Afraid that this was true, Hegazi asked one of the others, Mahmoud Mursi, to help him to persuade Waheeda to remain silent about the rape.

When Hegazi and Mursi found Waheeda again in the desert dark; it soon became clear the girl had absolutely no intention of remaining silent about the rape. She would report it as soon as she got home.

98

Angry again, Hegazi and Mursi tied her up despite her struggles then worried that her screams would attract attention, slit her throat and stabbed her several times. The rest of the group, standing some distance away, saw what happened and although horrified, they did nothing.

It was clear they could not leave the dying girl in full view of any passer-by, so the body was buried in the desert, everyone helping to scoop out a hole.

The initial police investigation into the disappearance of Waheeda Ghanem around the Deaf school had frightened Hegazi and Mursi into taking a car belonging to Murzi's father back out to the spot where they had buried the body three nights earlier. They dug up the body, wrapped it in a sheet, and drove with it in the boot of the car back through Cairo and over the river Nile into Giza near the pyramids where they dumped the body (minus the sheet) into a canal off-shoot of the Nile.

True enough, when the police investigation team went to the place where they were told the body had been buried, they found nothing in the shifting desert sand and they were unable to move the investigation on or make progress.

It is amazing to think that the body floated out of the canal into the main River Nile, and over 50 kilometres down the river to the pumping house without being spotted by anyone for three weeks, and that it was just luck the pumping house, normally deserted, was undergoing maintenance on the day the body floated by and seen by the maintenance workers who fished it out of the river.

A canal off-shoot of the River Nile at Giza where
Waheeda was thrown in by the murderers.

When Hegazi and Murzi appeared in court, their
defence attorney Muhammed Al Busaary alleged that
they had been tortured and their confessions forced
out of them. This cut no ice with the judge who
sentenced the two men to be hanged.

There were amazing scenes in the Supreme Court
in March 2000 when the death sentences were handed
out. Over 100 deaf people from Cairo staged a
demonstration in the court to show, they said, their
feelings over the rape and murder of Wahedda
Ghanem.

The police had to call in the security forces to break
up the demonstration and it was found that 17 of the
protestors were carrying knives! They were all arrested
and given minor sentences for carrying offensive
weapons in a government building!

The Supreme Court in Cairo where over 100 Deaf
people staged a demonstration protesting the rape
and murder of Waheeda Ghanem.

Deaf demonstrators in the
Cairo Supreme Court

Ahmed Hegazi and Mahmoud Murzi were re-tried on a technicality in April 2002 and their sentences were commuted to life imprisonment with a minimum of 25 years to be served before any parole could be considered.

Of the other three men and two women present at the murder and who did nothing, one woman named Sahar turned state evidence and described to the court what happened on the night Hegazi raped and killed Waheeda Ghanem. She was given a one-year prison term, and the three young men received 8-year prison sentences for "assisting in the disposal of a crime victim". The other young girl was a juvenile and was dealt with by a lower court.

The author and his wife, Maureen, with Mohammed Ahmed, a Deaf man in Cairo who provided details of this story.

Chapter 14

2000: West Yorkshire, England

The Man who got lost on the way to a Murder!

When the body of Alan Clark was discovered in his house in Carlton Road, Barnsley on 8 November 2000 by two colleagues from an employment agency who were concerned when he failed to turn up for work, the subsequent post mortem indicated he had been dead between 24-36 hours.

The scene inside the house was particularly gory, with blood splattered all over the ground floor. These, together with numerous cuts on the victim's hand, indicated there had been a fierce struggle in which the victim had fought for his life. It was clear that at one stage, he had tried to hide in an understairs cupboard, only to be dragged out and the attack continued.

The murder was extensively reported in the local media and this prompted several people to come forward and provide information to the police about a middle-aged male of Asian or Arabic origin who kept asking for directions to Carlton Road.

It did not take the police long to find that the victim was in a relationship with a senior manager of the same employment agency in Sheffield where he worked; they went to interview her and discovered she was separated from an Egyptian-born man living in Nottingham.

At the end of the day on 9 November 2000, police announced in a press statement that they had arrested a Deaf man aged 38 named Sarwat Al-Assaf on suspicion of murdering Alan Clark, his estranged wife's lover.

Alan Clark,
murdered in a frenzied attack

Sarwat Al-Assaf was born in Cairo, Egypt on 4 July
1962. One of for children, at the age of three he
suffered a severe head injury from a balcony. This is
stated to have resulted in profound bilateral hearing
loss. From the age of five he received specialist
education at The Cairo School for the Deaf in Egypt,
moving to a school in Lebanon at the age of seven and
later returning to Egypt. At school, he was interested in
all types of sports and had many friends with whom he
socialised. Moving to England at the age of nineteen,

Sarwat Al-Assaf attended the Royal School for the Deaf in Derby and then technical college, leaving at the age of twenty-three with a qualification in electrical engineering. Thereafter Sarwat Al-Assaf was employed in a variety of occupations, although not all of them used this qualification.

Sarwat Al-Assaf learnt to communication in BSL at Derby. This was to become his main means of communication. He was particularly close to his brother Samir Al-Assaf, who also lived in England during part of the 1990's. Communication between the two of them developed as a unique sign language during their childhood and it was clear that they understood each other well.

There was a first marriage in 1985 and had two children were born. One child, a son now aged eighteen, lived with Sarwat Al-Assaf's mother in Egypt. The other child died as a result of cot death after his birth in 1988.

Sarwat Al-Assaf met his second wife, Susan, in 1993. They lived together from 1994 and their daughter was born in 1995. Following his divorce in February 1997, they married in March 1997. Mrs Al-Assaf, who was not Deaf, communicated with her husband using BSL although she was less proficient at the language than him.

The marriage began to experience difficulties when, despite being in employment, Sarwat Al-Assaf started to accumulate large debts. Working night shifts, he was increasingly absent from home without explanation. It was only later that it became clear he had been gambling. At the time his wife expressed concern to their doctor that her husband sometimes seemed to be disorientated and talked of hearing a voice telling him to do things. Sometimes he did not remember where he lived and would seem to get lost. At home he was anxious and spoke of severe headaches. After being seen locally by a consultant neurologist in 1998, Sarwat Al-Assaf underwent a CT brain scan and an electroencephalogram. No significant abnormalities were found.

Sarwat Al-Assaf's debts reportedly reached £30,000 and involved him forging his wife's signature. Eventually the matrimonial home had to be sold to pay off the debts. For a while during 1999 the couple separated and lived in temporary accommodation. Early in 2000 they moved into their last home together, this being a house in Mrs Al-Assaf's sole name, but in August 2000 bailiffs arrived to remove Sarwat Al-Assaf's credit cards as a result of yet further debt.

On 20 September 2000 Mrs Al-Assaf informed her husband that she wished to end the marriage and that she wanted a divorce. In a state of distress Sarwat Al-Assaf tried to prevent her leaving the house, telling her that he would kill himself.

Sarwat Al-Assaf was so distressed that Susan Al-Assaf's parents and sister called an ambulance, and he was taken with his wife acting as interpreter, to the Accident and Emergency Department (AED) at the Queen's Medical Centre (QMC), Nottingham. En route, he remained distressed, confessing to gambling for the first time and speaking of a man whom he believed had been a bad influence on him in the past. He described this man as a bad person inside of him that he was trying to cut out. Mrs Al Assaf thought this person was probably imaginary.

At the QMC AED, he was seen in succession by a triage nurse, a senior house officer then a clinical nurse specialist from the Department of Psychological

Medicine who made the assessment that Sarwat Al-Assaf's *"... wife and daughter needed space away from him..."* due to his violence. The clinical nurse specialist also arranged for Sarwat Al-Assaf to be admitted to a psychiatric ward. Unfortunately the assessment notes and arrangements for admission got mislaid in the psychiatric ward so when the duty house officer in the psychiatric ward saw Sarwat Al-Assaf, there was a complete misunderstanding of what he was there for and he was allowed to walk out of the building, to the fury of Mrs. Al-Assaf who had interpreted for her husband throughout the time in the hospital. She stormed out of the hospital and complained bitterly no-one had listened to her and were only interested in her interpretation of the dialogue between husband and medical staff.

The Queen's Medical Centre, Nottingham housing the busiest Accident & Emergency department in Britain to which Sarwat Al-Assaf was taken for treatment and assessment

So, instead of having her husband placed in a psychiatric ward and having some space away from him, Susan Al-Assaf was forced to return home with her husband. The days that followed were a nightmare for her as her husband followed her around, several times stopping her leaving the house and causing her to feel frightened of him. He threatened suicide several times, made minor cuts on his wrists.

On Saturday 7 October, Susan Al-Assaf left home taking their daughter with her. She also informed her husband that she had formed a new relationship with a colleague in the Employment Agency where she worked. This information unhinged Sarwat Al-Assaf and it was made worse the next day, when she returned to the house to collect some clothes, and personal belongings. For her safety, she came accompanied by her new boyfriend, Alan Clark, her sister and her sister's boyfriend, but on seeing them, Sarwat Al-Assaf became distressed and later described his frustration at being unable to sign because his arms were held; "*not being able to tell them to stop, it just made me powerless*".

Mrs Al-Assaf felt very concerned about Sarwat Al-Assaf because he was so agitated. A few days earlier, he had slashed her car tyres and attempted to burn her car, so Susan Al Assaf fled and went into hiding. Sarwat Al-Assaf later went to his parents-in-law's house with a handwritten note stating "*I will go home by myself and set fire to my body*". Mrs Al-Assaf's sister called at Sarwat Al-Assaf's address where he told her he had poured petrol on himself. She telephoned Nottingham Social Services Emergency Duty Team reporting that Mrs Al-Assaf had fled, fearful of her husband's violence and reporting he had threatened her with a knife. Sarwat Al-Assaf was described as "*rigid with hysteria*". She was advised to contact his doctor for a psychiatric assessment. However, as Sarwat Al-Assaf had also threatened to set fire to himself and the house, pouring liquid over himself from a petrol can, the sister called the police. When tested, the liquid was found to be a mixture of water and petrol, but Sarwat Al-Assaf was taken by the police, with his agreement, back to QMC's AED, and subsequently to a bed in the psychiatric unit.

There, he underwent a series of assessments which concluded there would be no danger to Susan Al-Assaf and as there was no legal basis for detaining him in the hospital he was released on the proviso he kept regular appointments with a specialist psychiatric nurse for the deaf.

Sarwat's brother flew in from Egypt, and supported him in meetings with the psychiatric nurse, and also with his solicitor to ensure he had access to his daughter who was now back living in the family home with Susan Al-Assaf. Samir Al-Assaf tried to help him to accept that divorce from Susan was inevitable. On the surface, Sarwat Al-Assaf appeared to accept this but he was still harassing his ex-wife, sleeping in his car in the drive. A restraint order was considered against Sarwat Al-Assaf but his brother found him a place to stay in a hostel. Samir Al-Assaf was also able to settle some of the debts incurred by Sarwat, and feeling that things were now settling down, Samir returned to Egypt. After his brother had gone, Sarwat Al-Assaf took the opportunity to break his ex-wife's house in Chilwell, Nottingham, where he found a condom in the bedroom and a mislaid driving licence with the name and address of Alan Clark, who he now knew to be his ex-wife's lover. He photocopied the licence, then threw the real one into a refuse bin.

The result of his entry into his ex-wife's house was that his anger and resentment boiled over again, and on 6 November 2000, he told friends he was going to drive to Leicester, but instead, armed with a knife, he drove to Barnsley where Alan Clark, a 37-year old divorced father of one, lived to confront him. By not having a local A-Z street map, he became hopelessly lost trying to find Carlton Road.

He stopped at three garages, a fish & chip shop and finally, someone in the street, to ask for directions. His final contact, the person in the street, was able to direct him to the right road and subsequently remembered Sarwat Al-Assaf when news of the murder broke in the papers.

When he finally found the house, he confronted Alan Clark when the latter opened his front door to persistent ringing and banging. Alarmed at the confrontation, Clark tried to push Sarwat Al-Assaf off his doorstep and to close the front door but the Egyptian was in a rage and immediately launched a frenzied attack on his victim. The fight raged from the hallway through the lounge and back to the hallway where the victim tried to shut himself in a cupboard under the stairs, only to be dragged out again and hauled across the hallway into the kitchen where the body was eventually found by two of Mr. Clark's Employment Agency colleagues on the morning of 8 November.

The post-mortem on Alan Clark revealed that he had been stabbed at least 21 times. There were 4 wounds on the hands where he had tried to defend himself, 5 wounds on the neck and 12 wounds on the body itself. In addition, the post mortem revealed a clear image of a shoeprint on the victim's face which was later matched with Sarwat Al-Assaf's shoe.

Sarwat Al-Assaf cleaned himself up in the victim's kitchen, then drove back to Nottingham apparently unconcerned because the next day, he kept a pre-planned appointment with his specialist psychiatric nurse. During that appointment, he was calm and seemed to be much less stressed-out than he had been last time he saw the psychiatric nurse. He laughed off several scratches on his face, saying that he had walked into a large bush in the dark.

When he was arrested by the police and charged with Alan Clark's murder, he denied ever having been to Barnsley but three things told against him:

- The witnesses who gave him directions in Barnsley who all remembered him and his car.
- The shoeprint on Alan Clark's face.
- DNA belonging to Sarwat Al-Assaf that were recovered from underneath the victim's fingernails.

At his trial in Sheffield Crown Court, the jury rejected any suggestion that Sarwat Al-Assaf suffered from any mental disorder. The jury also rejected a plea of guilty to manslaughter on the grounds of diminished responsibility. After more than 8 hours deliberation, they found him guilty of the murder of Alan Clark.

Mr. Justice Pitchford sentenced Sarwat Al-Assaf to life imprisonment, saying "I have no doubt that you went to Mr. Clark's house prepared for violence. Mr. Clark had already indicated that he wished to have no confrontation with you."

The judge also referred to the forensic evidence provided by the police, "The evidence that you pursued him into a cupboard to continue your attack then dragged him out of it again into the kitchen to complete it was very compelling, and I agree with the jury's verdict."

The interior of Sheffield Crown
Court where Sarwat Al-Assaf
was sentenced to life
imprisonment.

Meanwhile, across the Atlantic, a similar situation concerning the mental health of a Deaf person was developing...

Chapter 15

2000: Florida, USA

Five Bodies in One House

When a school bus driver failed to turn up for work on Friday 20 October 2000, along with her sister who worked as a helper for disabled children on the school buses, the school sent two security officers to the sisters' house at Lakewood Drive, Seffner, near Tampa. The sisters were known as reliable employees and without contact from them, the school thought it incumbent to check and see if they needed help. On arrival at 11.30, they received no response from the house so they called the Hillsborough County Sheriff's Office and explained their concerns.

Two deputies were sent to investigate, and together with the security officers, approached the house again. Deputy Luke Caggiana peered through a garage window and saw that a man was crouched, pointing a gun at the door which one of the security officers was approaching.

"Gun!" Caggiana yelled, and immediately everyone backed off and a sheriff's emergency response team was called. Some neighbours who knew that the young man spotted by Deputy Caggiana was deaf offered to try to coax him out, but this was refused by the police.

At about 3 p.m., deputies fired tear gas into the one-storey, concrete-block building and the man emerged unarmed, offering no resistance. He was identified as 25-year-old Dexter Alonzo Levingston, who had a record of arrests in Hillsborough starting in 1995, mostly for petty theft, drunken driving and marihuana offences.

When the effects of the tear gas had dissipated, sheriff's deputies ventured into the house and discovered five bodies in various locations. All were dead and had either been shot or had multiple stab wounds.

Hillsborough Sheriff's Sergeant Rod Reder said it was one of the deadliest crimes in county history. "I can't remember five bodies at one location before," he said.

Relatives of some of the slain family are held back by police officers at the scene

Stunned neighbours were not surprised that Dexter Levingston had been taken into custody.

"Every time I saw that young man," said one, "I just knew something was wrong with him. I passed him the other night when he was outside smoking and I got the chills from the look in his eye."

Police officials later disclosed the identities of the five people who were found in the house though they refused to say how each person died. *(Four years later, police still have not specified exactly how each person was killed. Autopsy reports plus other papers such as forensic reports and witness statements have been sealed by the courts).* Sheriff's deputies would only say that a variety of weapons were used, including guns, a machete, a knife, a screwdriver and a pair of scissors.

"It was a charnel house," said one deputy. Forensic experts took over a week to go through the house collecting evidence.

Forensic police officers collecting
evidence from the scene

The victims were named as:

- Nancy Marlins, aged 57, the owner of the home and Dexter Levingston's grandmother. She worked as a school bus helper for disabled children.
- Lillie Cacciamani, aged 56, Marlin's sister. She worked as a school bus driver.
- Barry Cacciamani, aged 47. He was white and the second husband of Lillie.
- Connie Carter, aged 40, Lillie's daughter from a previous relationship.
- Michele Murtha, a white 12-year-old girl with learning difficulties who was in the family's care. Local authorities were unsure of Marlins' relationship to Murtha who attended the Dover Elementary School. A spokesman for Florida's Department of Children and Families said that Nancy Marlins was not registered as a foster parent and the department had no record of the girl.

Dexter Levingston who worked occasionally for a neighbour whose family owned the Rigatoni Italian Eatery, was described as a nice guy but with a suspect temperament. He had a record of mental health problems. He could neither use the recognised form of American Sign Language nor speak but communicated through basic gestures.

Neighbours stated that they had detected some tension between Levingston and Barry Cacciamani but were unable to be specific about it.

Levingston was subsequently charged with the gruesome murders of his grandmother, great-aunt, great-uncle, a cousin and an unrelated disabled girl in his grandmother's care. However, the authorities were unable to move on from there because no-one, not even his mother and stepfather, were able to determine what was going on in his head or effectively communicate with him.

Consequently, on 14 February 2001, Hillsborough County Circuit Judge Chet Tharpe ordered that Dexter Levingston be sent to the state mental hospital at Chattahoochee to determine his competence to defend himself against five murder charges.

The next court action linked with this case took place not in the criminal court of Hillsborough County Circuit but in the civil court when a lawsuit was filed on behalf of Patricia Murtha and her husband (Michele Murtha's mother and stepfather). This alleged negligence by the state's Department of Children and Families (DCF) in placing a child in need of care in the home of an unregistered carer and for failing to carry out background checks on the people living in the house.

"The first and only time I visited Mrs. Marlins' house where Michele was staying, I saw a man washing a car outside," Patricia Murcha told reporters. She complained to the DCF about an inappropriate adult male living in the same house as a mentally disabled girl, but was reassured everything was okay.

A few weeks later, Michele Murcha was one of the five people killed by Dexter Levingston.

In the lawsuit, Michele Murtha's parents sued the DCF and two companies, claiming they failed to protect their mentally disabled girl.

Filed in Hillsborough Circuit Court, the lawsuit says the DCF, the Human Services Foundation Inc, and the Family Preservation Services of Florida Inc, should have better monitored the home run by carer Nancy Marlins. It sought millions in damages for pain and suffering.

"Something went wrong here", attorney Richard Hirsch said "Common sense tells you that you don't place a handicapped 12-year-old child in a private home without any support and with family members coming and going at will, one of whom has a criminal record."

The DCF contracted through the companies to have Marlins, 57-year-old school bus aide, care for the girl. But the state failed to inform the Murthas that Marlins wasn't licensed as a carer and failed to perform criminal background checks on the people staying in the home, Hirsh said. Levingston had a criminal record and a history of mental instability, according to the suit.

However, in August 2003, a judge declared a mistrial in the lawsuit after Michele's mother, Patricia, became too distraught to carry on after very aggressive questioning by the DCF's defence attorneys.

"Basically", said Patricia Murcha's attorney Richard Hirsch, "the state says Mrs Murcha had made a choice to abandon her daughter to Ms. Marlins."

However, the parents' argument was that they wanted Michele to have residential care and only allowed their daughter to live with Nancy Marlins on the state's assurance that it would be a temporary measure until a vacancy became available in a group home. Ms. Marlins was alleged to have taken other children into her home before on behalf of the DCF.

Although the lawsuit remains on file, it has not yet come back to court for a new trial.

Dexter Levingston

Meanwhile, Dexter Levingston had a competency hearing in October 2004 and was declared fit to stand trial. However, the case has still (as at April 2006) not come to trial and it is doubtful if it ever will.

Levingston has been returned to Hillsborough County jail whilst prosecutors and defence attorneys argue over the trial. Complications arise because prosecutors have made it clear they will demand the death penalty, and it is not the accepted practice in the

United States that a person with a history of mental disorders be given the death penalty.

Chapter 16

2001: Hebei, China

The Bomber

Between 4 o'clock and 5 o'clock on Friday morning 16 March 2001, a series of explosions rocked the city of Shijiazhuang in China's Hebei province, totally demolishing a number of buildings causing numerous deaths.

Shijiazhuang is the centre of China's textile industry located about 180 miles south-west of Beijing. A major railway hub, the city had recently gone through a period of unrest due to problems in the city's cotton mills and it was thought at first that the explosions were the work of disgruntled employees angry about the lay-offs and conditions in the cotton mills.

Police revised their views when they realised that all the locations targeted by bombs were workers dormitories, and after further investigation, they issued a Most Wanted poster bearing the photograph of a deaf man, Jin Ruchao, described as a 41-year-old unemployed worker who was already wanted for the murder of a woman discovered in China's southern province of Yunnan. A reward of 50,000 yuan (approximately £3,100/US$6000) was offered for the capture of Ruchao, and a further 100,000 yuan for clues to those who provided the explosives used in the bombing. The issue of the wanted poster was the start of the biggest manhunt ever undertaken in China.

121

In their attempts to catch Jin Ruchao, police throughout China stopped all trains between provinces, set up road blocks and searched vehicles on major roads and searched all hotels and guest houses.

The information released by the police indicated that Jin Ruchao was a deaf man who communicated mainly by written notes. It stated the motive for the bombing was revenge as all buildings targeted were places where his ex-wife, ex-mother-in-law and stepmother all lived.

The first buildings targeted were Apartment Buildings nos. 15 and 16 at Shijiazhuang's No. 3 Cotton Mill. Ruchao used to live in Building No. 16, and Building No. 15 was where his stepmother lived.

Other buildings targeted were elsewhere in the city where his ex-wife's parents and ex-wife and her new husband lived, plus a building that used to belong to his mother.

The information posters also indicated that Ruchao was wanted for other crimes as well. Although it was not specifically stated on the poster, this referred to the murder on 9 March of Wei Zhihua, a woman he had lived with for three months until she left him over his abuses, and returned to her home town in Maguan County, Yunnan.

It was also stated that Jin Ruchao had a conviction for rape in 1988, for which he served a 10-year prison sentence.

Apparently Ruchao had also been a former employee of Cotton Mill No. 3, until 1983 when he was dismissed for hooliganism. However, he kept a room in the factory's dormitory block No. 16, which was the building most severely affected. It was totally demolished. Altogether, 108 bodies were recovered from the bombed buildings, with 38 people seriously injured as to warrant hospital treatment. There were no reports or indications as to whether Ruchao's stepmother and father (who lived in Building no. 15), or the neighbours he had disputes with in Building no. 16, or his ex-wife's parents in another building, and his ex-wife plus new husband in a fourth building were killed in the explosions.

Two scenes showing the devastation caused by the bomb explosions in Shijiazhuang. The building on the left is all that is left of Building No. 16.

Left: Two mourners at one of the bomb sites

The nationwide search for Ruchao paid off in the early hours of Friday 23 March, exactly one week after the murders. Acting on a tip-off, police raided a guest house in Beihai, a beach resort in south-east China bordering Vietnam that was notorious for smuggling activities. They found that they had missed Ruchao by literally minutes and he was soon spotted riding a stolen motor-cycle, and a chase developed through what was left of the night for several hours before the suspect was cornered and arrested, and put on a plane to be returned to Shijiazhuang.

Jin Ruchao being returned
after his arrest for
interrogation

It was said by people that fifteen years ago, it would have been impossible for Ruchao to get the 1,200 miles from Shijiazhuang to Beihai without being stopped, and wondered whether a deaf man with no knowledge of explosives was being made a scapegoat for the bombings, and whether they were really the work of disgruntled employees.

However, police released information after the first interrogation of Ruchao that gave the following facts and events subsequent to the arrest:

1. Ruchao was motivated by hatred of his ex-wife, and her family and also his stepmother.
2. Ruchao had according to his sister "played" with explosives from an early age, and was experienced in their manufacture.
3. The sister had lent Ruchao the money that enabled him to travel to Yunnan. She had not known he was out for revenge and that he was going there to murder Wei Zhihua.
4. Ruchao bought a large amount of explosives from a man named Wang Yushun (who had been arrested) on 12 March for approximately £60.
5. Around 2 a.m. on 16 March, Ruchao had hired a man to help him to move 6 sacks of explosives to Building no. 16, and after he had left, Ruchao worked alone distributing the sacks around the building and adjacent building no. 15.
6. After he set a timer to detonate the explosives, he took a taxi ride to the home of his ex-wife's parents and at 4.30 a.m. detonated two bags of explosives he had previously secreted there. He then took another taxi ride to a dormitory building where his ex-wife and new husband lived, and set off two more bags of explosives at 4.45 a.m. He also set off explosives at a nearby building previously owned by his mother but had been sold by his sister. He was unhappy that his share of the sale proceeds was only 10,000 yuan (£620/US$1,200)

125

7. Police had also arrested Hao Fenqin and Hu Xiaohong for assisting in the supply of explosives.

Police said there was no doubt that Jin Ruchao was solely responsible for the deaths of 108 people in the series of bombings.

Jin Ruchao being interrogated by
writing

After a brief appearance in Shijiazhuang People's Court on 18 April, Jin Ruchao was sentenced to death by firing squad (China's usual method of execution).

Three others, Wang Yushun, Hao Fenqin and Hu Xiaohong, were also sentenced to be executed with him. The first two men were accused of selling Ruchao ammonia nitrate, and Hu Xiaohong was convicted of selling Ruchao 50 detonators and 20 paper fuses.

All four men were shot to death on 2 May 2001.

Jin Ruchao has the distinction of being the deaf person who has murdered the highest number of people – 109 (108 by bombing, and one by stabbing).

Chapter 17

2002: St. Augustine, Florida, USA

The Family Man who wanted more sex

When Carmen Maria Reyes had not been seen or heard from for at least 4 days, a relative went to her house at 419 Del Monte Drive opposite St. Augustine High School. What she found caused her to run screaming to a neighbour's house with a request to dial 911 and report a murder. Police responded quickly and were at the scene at 8.35 a.m. on 16 October 2002 when they discovered the body of Carmen Reyes.

Sheriff's deputies were quick off the mark responding to the 911 call to Carmen Reyes house

Born in Arecibo, Puerto Rico in 1976 into a family of two sisters and two brothers, all of whom had left their home island and settled in either St. Augustine or in South Carolina, Carmen Reyes had been born Deaf and additionally suffered from Ushers Syndrome, a form of progressive genetic disorder that combines progressive blindness (retinitis pigmentosa) with deafness

Her family had moved from Puerto Rico to St. Augustine initially because the city housed the Florida State School for the Deaf and Blind, and Carmen was enrolled into this school in 1986.

The Florida School for the Deaf and Blind,
St. Augustine; the victim (and her killer) both
attended this school

Police investigators spent all day inside the house collecting evidence and the body of the victim was not removed from the house until late afternoon when it was taken away for an autopsy.

Details of the cause of her death was controlled by the St. John's County Sheriff Office's violent Crimes Unit because they wanted this information held back until the case went to a grand jury or to a trial jury.

Sergeant Charles Mulligan of the Sheriff's Office said "At the end of this criminal investigation, we want to finalize it with a successful prosecution of the perpetrator".

Residents in the locality were stunned by the murder, the first in the neighbourhood in living memory.

Two weeks into the investigation, police announced the arrest of a Deaf man named Joshua Raymond Wolfe. The police investigation had begun to focus upon him when detectives learnt from witnesses that his car had been seen parked outside the victim's house around the time of the murder. Tips also came into the Sheriff's Office from the St. Augustine deaf community, some of which said that Wolfe had spoken of the killing.

Wolfe was asked to come into the Sheriff's Office voluntarily and was arrested after being questioned by Detective Howard Cole. At the start of the session, the suspect denied killing Reyes but Cole informed him the police had recovered evidence that suggested he was at the murder house the night Reyes was killed.

"Wolfe hung his head and began to cry," Detective Cole subsequently wrote in his report.

Joshua Raymond Wolfe was aged 22, married with a little boy and worked as a stock clerk in Publix, an employee-owned supermarket chain, in the Ponto Vedra Beach area of St. Augustine. Wolfe was also a former student of Florida State School for the Deaf, and had known Carmen Reyes from his school days although they had not been in the same class. Reyes had been at the school from 1986 to 1995, and Wolfe from 1991 to 1998, but failed to graduate. He lived with his wife in a converted garage apartment in Jacksonville Beach, his wife's parents living in a house in front of the garage.

Former teachers and classmates of Wolfe from the Florida School for the Deaf and Blind expressed shock at the arrest, but one said that Wolfe did get angry easily and tended to be physically aggressive as he became angry.

"But I never thought he would be capable of something like that," one teacher said.

A spokesman from the Sheriff's Office told reporters that Wolfe had tried to alter evidence at the crime scene but technicans from the Florida Department of Law Enforcement were able to gather sufficient evidence in spite of this to nail Wolfe.

In the last days of 2002, the State of Florida filed notice that they would seek the death penalty for the first-degree murder of Carmen Maria Reyes. Assistant State Attorney Maureen Christine said that the circumstances surrounding the killing were particularly atrocious and warranted the death penalty.

It was August 2003 before the depositions were heard before the court and the trial, originally docketed for October 2003 was moved back several times as Wolfe's defence attorneys fought the District Attorney's office with plea bargaining over the death penalty and with competency hearings.

Three days before his trial, Wolfe surprised his defence team with a last minute decision to accept a plea agreement by plead guilty to first-degree murder. By doing this, he avoided a death sentence should a guilty verdict be returned against him in trial.

Joshua Raymond Wolfe

Instead, the 18 July 2005 court session was given over to a review of the indictment and impostion of a life sentence.

The court heard that Carmen Maria Reyes was found on her kitchen floor. Wolfe claimed to have been engaged in a secret affair with Reyes but the court was told the most likely scenario was that Wolfe went to Reyes house with the intention of having sex but when Reyes refused, he lost his temper and battered her.

Because of Reyes' Usher's Sydrome, she would have been helpless, finding it difficult to pinpoint where Wolfe was in the room. He raped her in her living room and also in her bedroom before falling asleep. Upom waking up, he realised Reyes was dead. Sometime during the rape and battering, he had stabbed her.

In a slight panic, he tried to clean up the crime scene by wiping door knobs and surfaces where he might have left fingerprints. He also found a Clorox bottle (a type of bleach) and poured it in Reyes' mouth, genitals and stomach. He threw away some of his clothing in a trash bin, then drove the 30 miles home to Jacksonville Beach where he took a long shower.

Joshua Wolfe said he was sorry for killing Reyes and knew he deserved to be punished for what he had done. He wanted to be put in prison and left alone.

He got his wish when he was sentenced to life without the possibility of parole.

Chapter 18

2003: Worthing, England

A Killing Fuelled by Cider

When a woman has a relationship with one man then leaves him for one of his friends, trouble is bound to follow if the three of them still go around together and spend all day drinking cider. This is what happened when June Fleming[1] left Robert Morris, an unemployed 41-year old landscape gardener who was also a profoundly deaf sign language user, and moved in with his friend, Grant Flame, aged 44, a divorced father of three.

On 24 January 2003, Flame and Fleming went to Morris's flat on Worthing's Broadwater estate with bottles of cider and spent the day watching television, boozing and generally arguing about the current state of the nation, including the Iraq war. At around 8p.m. that evening, Fleming rather loudly and drunkenly asked Flame how they were going to get home with no money for either bus or taxi. This developed into a loud row with each blaming the other for spending all their money on the cider.

In order to stop the row, Morris suggested that Fleming sleep off her drunkenness on the sofa, but Flame would have to leave and walk home.

---

[1] June Fleming is not the real name of the person concerned. She has been given a different name to protect her identity.

According to Morris, Grant Flame took a serious objection to this suggestion, assuming that Morris had intended to have sexual intercourse with Fleming, his ex-girlfriend. Perhaps Flame was afraid that Fleming would leave him and return to Morris. In any event, Flame is alleged to have attacked Morris, punching him several times and trying to strangle him.

In the struggle, Morris picked up a craft knife and used it to slash Grant Flame's throat. When that happened, Flame staggered to his feet and blundered out of Morris's ground floor flat next door to the Oasis Centre, before collapsing in the hallway leading to the street where he was found by an elderly resident living in the same block of flats.

The murder scene taped off for investigation by forensic experts

The resident called an ambulance but Grant Flame was dead when the paramedics reached him. The police who were called to the scene only had to follow the trail of blood straight to Morris's flat. On admission to the flat, they found Morris covered in blood. Fleming was weeping uncontrollably and also splattered with blood.

Both Morris and Fleming were immediately arrested by police officers and taken to the local police station. June Fleming was later released after it became clear she had not been involved in the killing, but Morris was charged with murder and appeared at Worthing Magistrates Court on Monday 27 January where he pled not guilty through a sign language interpreter.

In a 9-day trial at Lewes Crown Court in October 2003, Robert Morris re-enacted the attack by Grant Flame, using his own armchair which had been brought into court for demonstration purposes. He said that:

"I was trying to pull him off to stop him throttling me. I was struggling to get free. I grabbed the knife. I thought the knife would make him back off. With

Morris, covered by the customary blanket, is led into Court

Grant Flame

all the drink, if I had given him the chance, he probably would have killed me".

"Grant was really strangling me and I couldn't judge the distance between where Grant's head was and my arm. It was a desperate act to make him back off".

Using a pen, Morris demonstrated how he brandished the knife and said he never meant to cut

135

Flame's throat: "I just wanted him to let go and it just went across. It was unlucky it just went across his throat".

However, the prosecution described the killing as brutal and said that whatever had happened in the flat that night there was no dispute that Grant Flame had been left dying in a pool of blood and Robert Morris had done nothing at all to keep him.

The jury agreed and returned as unanimous verdict of guilty after less than three hours deliberation.

Robert Morris was sentenced to life imprisonment.

Chapter 19

2003: London, England

Cash for Drugs Led to Murder

When drug addicts become desperate for money to buy more drugs and sustain their habit, they will do anything to get the money for fair means or foul, whether by stealing things, burglary, prostitution or even murder!

When Nabeel Aljubori walked the three-quarter mile from his dingy flat in Kempt Street, Plumstead to Derek Dale's equally seedy flat in Arthur Grove not far from the Woolwich Arsenal, it was because he was desperate to get more drugs to feed his habit. Aljubori was extremely disappointed to find that the 16-year-old Dale did not have any drugs either.

Both Aljubori, who was 22, and Dale had mental health problems and had become friends through their drug habit and also through meeting up at the Bracton Centre in Dartford for their treatments. They were an odd couple; Aljubori was a Yemeni Arab who had hebephrenic schizophrenia, which is marked by delusion and hallucinations; Dale was Deaf, a school drop-out and had learning difficulties.

Both young men decided they needed some cash to purchase drugs so on the night of 18-19 June 2003, both set out to break into a number of houses around the estate where Derek Dale lived. In this area bordered by Invermore Place, Burrage Road, Sandbach Place and Dale's own street, Arthur Grove, they went on an all-night rampage breaking into whatever houses or flats took their fancy.

In some places, they were seen and chased off but in one flat, they stole a computer and some games which they decided was not enough to buy them the drugs they needed.

It was then that Derek Dale suggested they go and rob a man they both knew who was also a patient at the Bracton Centre and with whom Dale had previously smoked cannabis in the other man's flat.

Nabeel Aljubori thought it was a really good idea, so they went to the flat of Paul Geddes in Dawson Close, which was actually the next street to Arthur Grove where Dale lived. Their two flats were practically back-to-back.

However, when they got into Paul Geddes' flat at 6 a.m. on the morning of 19 June, they were disappointed to find that he had no drugs, no money and nothing worth stealing. Enraged, they attacked their 32-year-old victim, bashing his head. They also stamped on his ribs, breaking several of them and paid particular attention to Geddes' genitals, severely bruising them and causing a haemorrhage in the scrotum. Finally they cut off one ear and tried to cut off the other as well.

Paul Geddes' pleas for mercy were ignored, and once they had vented their anger on their victim, they exited the flat, leaving him to die. However, their shouting and banging at 6 a.m. had annoyed a neighbour who observed them leave.

Paul Geddes, aged 32, had not worked since 1989 and was receiving medication for mental health problems. Neighbours described him as eccentric but harmless, a vulnerable man who was easily taken advantage of.

Later that evening, having failed to find any more money, they returned to Geddes' flat, poured petrol over his dead body and furnishings, and set fire to them. It was the fire fighters called out to attend to the fire that found his body and called the police who were appalled by the extent of the injuries suffered by Geddes.

It was quite easy for the police to discover from various neighbours the activities and the identities of the two men. People on the estate might have been annoyed about the burglary attempts by Dale and Aljubori without really bothering to inform the police, but the particularly barbarous murder of a vulnerable and eccentric young man with mental health problems was an entirely different matter and they quickly provided the information that led to the attest of Derek Dale and Nabeel Aljubori.

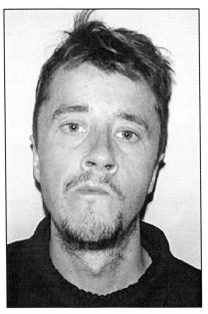

Paul Geddes

The matter was clinched for the police when they found a Burberry coat in Aljubori's possession that had fire damage.

At their trial at the Old Bailey in December 2004, the jury learnt from witnesses the extent of Paul Geddes' horrific injuries and heard Prosecutor Victor Temple, Q.C. say that "... the defendants were seeking money or property which could be converted into cash to buy drugs. They were so driven in their pursuit they carried on, even when they had been seen by potential witnesses."

Derek Dale was found guilty of murder and sentenced to life imprisonment, with a minimum tariff of 15 years before he could be considered for parole.

Judge Peter Fingret told him: "This was a particularly brutal and callous murder on a mild and inoffensive young man. You and your co-defendant beat him to death, in the course of which you severed one of his ears and attempted to do the same with the other. It is hard to believe human beings can behave in such a way to their fellow man."

Nabeel Aljubori was cleared of murder but convicted of manslaughter and referred to Southwark Crown Court for sentencing following compilation of psychiatric reports.

On Tuesday 22 March 2005, Judge Fingret was urged by a consultant psychiatrist from the Bracton Centre to lock up Aljubori indefinitely as he was a danger to the public.

The judge informed Aljubori that he had been convicted of manslaughter, not murder, on grounds of diminished responsibility but he was to be sentenced to be locked away in a mental hospital indefinitely.

Chapter 20

2004: Neath, South Wales

The Tuckshop Murder

Spending all afternoon in the local British Legion Club in front of the widescreen TV watching Wales storm to victory over Scotland 23-10 in the European Six Nations Rugby Championships can be a good way of enjoying oneself, but not, perhaps, to the point of almost drinking oneself senseless with six pints of beer and three shots of vodka, particularly if one is under the legal age for alcohol and unable to control his drink. This is what happened to a seventeen-year-old Welsh lad who was in the British Legion with his father and older brother.

Realising he had no money left for his bus fare home, the young lad asked his brother for the loan of a few pounds but his brother was hard up himself and could only give the other just enough to cover the bus fare.

Getting up to leave British Legion, the young lad fell over a stool on his way to the toilet then staggered out of the club. Once out in the cold February air, the young lad sobered slightly and looking at the money in his hand, he decided it was not enough. Although he was only 17, he had a history of convictions for minor misdemeanours and robbery. This included the assault on a police officer, a schoolboy who refused to hand over his lunch money, a woman who refused to let him "borrow" her van and a woman he had robbed in the street, so the most obvious thing for him to do was to go out and rob someone to provide himself with funds.

An afternoon's drinking watching the Wales v. Scotland rugby game caused a young man to go short of money.

Meanwhile, not far away in her home in Bryn Terrace in the same village of Melincourt, near Neath, 76-year-old widow Delcie Winstone was resting in her back room. In a throwback to the 1940s and 1950s, Mrs Winstone ran what was known as a 'tuckshop' in her front parlour. In this room, she sold sweets, chocolates, and soft drinks to local children at cost prices, doing it for enjoyment rather than for a living.

She had no shop counter, just a trestle table; no cash register, just a few old ice cream tubs in which she kept her change. She had been doing this for over 20 years and was well-known to generations of children.

Howard Winstone

Despite her age, Delcie Winstone was a fit, feisty character whose cousin (now deceased) was former world featherweight boxing champion, Howard Winstone.

The drunken young lad was one of those who knew of the tuckshop. He guessed that the old lady would have money in her tuckshop and decided to go and rob her.

After knocking on the door, he waited until Mrs. Winstone had opened it then asked her if he could buy a bar of chocolate. Despite it being after six o'clock and dark, Mrs. Winstone recognised him and let him into her front parlour shop. Whilst the old lady's back was turned getting him the chocolate he had asked for, he grabbed the small change she kept in her ice cream tubs but she heard him.

"She started shouting at him, kicked me in the leg and slapped me", he said in a police statement after he had been arrested. "I kind of lost it. It was a shock. I thought she was a nice old lady. She'd never slapped me before when I was a child."

The 17-year-old admitted that the slap and kick caused him to lose his temper and hit out with his fists. As Mrs. Winstone staggered back into a corner, he hit her a third and fourth time. As she fell, she clung to his leg so he hit her some more and as she lay on the floor, he stamped on her.

Delcie Winstone

As the red mists of his temper lifted from him, he was horrified at what he had done. This did not, however, stop him from raiding the ice cream tubs and taking £30 of petty cash. He also found £100 in notes in a wallet on her person. He then noticed with some distaste that he had blood on his shoes, and went into the kitchen to try to wash if off but only succeeded in making the mess worse so he exited the house.

There was still the matter of trying to get home and outside, he spotting Mrs. Winstone's Peugeot 106 car. Going back into the house, he found the keys to the car, and climbed in. He did not know how to drive very well, though, and his revving of the engine attracted the attention of a neighbour, a local butcher, who ran outside to try to stop the car being driven off.

After a few yards, the car stalled and the neighbour was able to snatch the keys out of the car. He was less successful in detaining the youth who broke free of him and ran off into the night. Concerned about Delcie Winstone, the neighbour went into her house. One look at the state of the front parlour where the struggle had been taken place told him it was necessary to call in the police.

Police responded within a few minutes and discovered the body of Delcie Winstone in her blood-spattered tuckshop. It did not take the police long to home in onto the 17-year-old youth and arrest him later the same night, 14 February 2004.

The next day during a search of his house, the youth's bloodstained white T-shirt was found behind a bath panel.

Because of his age, an order banning identification of him in the media was made when he was charged with the murder of Delcie Winstone.

At Swansea Crown Court in July 2004, the 17-year-old denied robbing and murdering Delcie Winstone but admitted theft and manslaughter. The court heard that the victim had been repeatedly struck on the head near the trestle table on which she laid out sweets and soft drinks for sale.

Forensic police experts prepare to search the victim's house for evidence.

Forensic scientist Claire Galbraith who examined the shop after Mrs. Winstone was found told the court she found several types of blood marks.

She said there was "impact spatter" indicating a blow into wet blood and contact marks where blood was smeared against a wall. There were also blood spots on the sweets and drinks which Mrs. Winstone had on display and on plastic cartons she used to keep cash in.

She concluded after examining bloodstaining in the shop that: "A confrontation had taken place during which Mrs. Winstone was stuck a number of blows and used her arms and hands to defend herself. Some had caused bruising and others bleeding."

"The likely scenario is that she was moving around in the confined corner near a radiator in the room. Blood patterns support the view she was upright then began to fall downwards and as she stumbled around she was repeatedly hit before falling to the floor."

On 29 July 2004, the jury of nine men and three women unanimously returned verdicts of guilty of murder and a separate charge of robbery against the youth. On receiving the verdicts, the judge Mr. Justice Pitchford lifted the order banning the identification of the youth, who was revealed to be Dwayne Evans of Clyne in the next village from Melincourt.

Dwayne Evans

Dwayne Evans had been Deaf since he was a baby after contacting meningitis and relied on British Sign Language as his principle means of communication.

He had more or less dropped out of school at 15 when he began to drink heavily and commit serious assault offences.

Giving evidence in BSL to the court, Evans said he had become upset and disorientated after Mrs. Winstone had slapped him. When he looked down at the body after he had battered her, he had punched himself in the head and said, "God, what have I done? I'm stupid!"

Sentencing Evans to life imprisonment with a minimum of 8 years to be served, plus 2½ years detention for the robbery, Mr. Justice Pitchford told Evans: "These convictions for murder and robbery represent a very serious escalation in your short criminal career. You have already shown yourself to be a violent and unpredictable young man. This time, your violent behaviour resulted in the death of Delcie Winstone in her own home, an offence which must continue to cause her relatives, her neighbours and friends shock and dismay".

Chapter 21

2005: Virginia, USA

Illegal Immigrant Trapped by DNA

Williamsburg, in the state of Virginia is called the cradle of the American dream. It's the place where American giants like George Washington, Thomas Jefferson and Patrick Henry started to oppose British rule. In 1699, Williamsburg was America's first city.

Nowadays, Williamsburg glorifies in its colonial past. It organise regular historic pageants and events, and has been to the forefront of restoring 18th century buildings, farms and other memorabilia to cater for its 4 million tourists every year.

Behind this façade, there is another Williamsburg, made up of a large number of trailer home parks that have a broad mix of poor white and immigrant people, many from Central American republics such as Mexico, El Salvador and Honduras.

Brittany Binger was one such poor white girl, living in a trailer park home with two other girls (sisters) and their mother. Brittany was 16 years old, a High School drop-out, the daughter of a bulldozer operator and a mini-mart shop worker. Both parents were divorced and Brittany was no longer in touch with either her father or her mother. Sisters Danielle Hollingsworth and Kristin Thurston, aged 18 and 22, and their mother had taken Brittany into their mobile home out of kindness.

On 2 Sunday January 2005, Brittany Binger finished her tea of macaroni and cheese, washed her dirty plate and crockery in the mobile home kitchenette and at 7.30 p.m., put on her coat, picked up her purse and with a cheery bye, bye to the two sisters, stepped out of the mobile home and set out to walk to another trailer home park that lay on the other side of a convenience store called Millers Mart and a bar called Y-B's. She was visiting somebody she was having a sexual relationship with and the two sisters did not expect to see her again until the next morning, The route that Brittany would take was a path between the two trailer home parks that ran behind Millers Mart and Y-B's.

Now, in jeans and white sneakers, she walked in the park past the bar and the mini-mart. She made it only a few hundred yards further, to a swath of grass at the Whispering Pines entrance. And as she lay there dead that night, no one missed her; the friend had not realised she was coming as she had not told him.

A newspaper carrier found her two hours before dawn on Monday. She was on the back, legs together, arms outstretched – "a crucifix position," police called it. Her sneakers were off and her jacket was unsnapped. Her T-shirt was hiked up exposing her breasts and her jeans were yanked down. The autopsy confirmed that she had been raped.

Brittany Binger

Someone had strangled her, likely from behind with an arm, while pressing his other hand over her nose and mouth, suffocating her. There was skin under her left-hand fingernails, meaning she almost certainly had scratched whoever killed her. She had died between 7.30 and 9.30 the night before.

Because her purse and most of its contents were scattered along the sidewalk, police surmised that the attacker had rifled through the purse as he fled, discarding things he didn't want. Detective bagged the belongings as evidence, along with some scattered trash, including a plastic juice bottle, which was nearly full. It was standing upright on a driveway 12 feet from the dead girl.

With all seven detectives from the local police force working the case, the investigation was moving in several directions when Margie Spencer arrived on Tuesday from the nearby Hampton Roads area. She and other members of a volunteer group travelled frequently with their tracking dogs, aiding law enforcement agencies all over the country. Patton, 5 years old, had been training since he was a puppy and was an excellent tracker.

"Find the man" Spencer commanded.

At the Whispering Pines entrance that afternoon, after a police officer rubbed a small gauze pad against Binger's jacket, Spencer had held the pad to Patton's nose. The dog registered the strongest scent that wasn't Binger's. And when he heard the order, he started tracking straining his leash, pulling Spencer behind him. He went first to Y-B's tavern and barked excitedly around the booth near the restrooms.

After the hound was done rooting in Y-B's, he followed the suspect's scent back out to the parking area. He nosed along the ground, leading Spencer and two police officers – Gibbs and Branch – past several shopfronts in the faded little plaza until they came to the convenience store, Millers Mart. Patton was as frantic there as he had been in the tavern, howling to be let in, then tracking to a drinks cooler, sniffing and pawing at the glass door.

So, the clues: someone whose fresh scent was on Binger's jacket most likely hung out in Y-B's and had sat in the booth by the restrooms, and had stopped in Millers Mart to get a drink from the vending cooler.

Many bar patrons had sat in that booth. Detectives decided to start by checking out those known to have sat there lately.

On Wednesday night, one of the investigators, Pat Murray saw "a Mexican guy" standing near Y-B's and asked him for identification. At first, Murray thought the man didn't speak English, but then he realized what the problem was. After the detective managed to get across what he wanted, the man motioned for him to follow, and they walked a short distance into the Windy Hill Park behind the bar.

When they reached a mobile home on Beckie Lane, just a block from where the victim had been staying, the detective waited as the man rummaged inside a shed. He came out with a government-issued ID card from El Salvador bearing his date of birth and name: Oswaldo Elias Martinez.

Murray jotted down the particulars. And before he left, he did one thing: Standing in the dark, he took out a camera and snapped a photo of Martinez's face

Detectives asked around about him and kept his name in mind – one of many names – as they hunted for Binger's killer through January and into February, investigation ex-boyfriends, estranged registered sex offenders and others, and searching in vain for drug or gang connections serious enough to result in homicide.

The search for the killer of Brittany Binger would go on for weeks. It was the biggest investigation in living memory for the small St. James City police force, which had only 73 officers, only seven of whom were detectives.

While investigators investigated many people, the "Mexican guy" featured quite a lot in their thoughts but they could not connect him to the killing.

"The Mexican guy" wasn't Mexican but a Salvadoran immigrant, Oswaldo Martinez, and he had just turned 33 at the time of the killing. A day labourer then 5-foot-4 and 130 pounds, with a thin moustache and black hair pulled into a short ponytail, he had been in the country illegally for about a year. And for weeks, before and after the murder of Brittany Binger, he was fixture in Y-B's.

"He was a lonely person, I think," said Tom Cail, 60, drinking beer one recent night with a half-dozen other customers of the bar.

Y-B's drew a working-class crowd, many of its regulars coming from trailer parks nearby. They showed up their lunch hours and after quitting time – women with sore hands and tired feet, men in NASCAR ball caps and old jeans, their fingernails rimmed with factory grime. They drank Bud in bottles for $2.15, drafts for $1.25, and lounged or shot pool while the jukebox played country-and-western.

Cail and his friends said that Martinez started showing up in November. Because he had nothing to say to people, most folks stopped wondering what his story was and just accepted him as part of the scenery. They figured he didn't speak English.

Being a foreigner, he seemed socially clueless. He sometimes propositioned women by waving to get their attention, pointing to himself, then pursing his lips and making kissing sounds. They laughed him off. Mostly, he sat quietly, and on the few occasions when people tried to talk with him, he said nothing.

153

When he wanted a beer, he'd show waitress Carol Howard his hands, one above the other – close together for a draft, farther apart for a bottle. If he flashed six fingers, she'd bring him a half-dozen fried dumplings. If he wanted a burger, he'd cup his hands as if he were about to bite into one. He never acted drunk and, except for his occasional leering at women, he never got out of line in the bar.

"For a long time, he'd just sit over there and stare," said one woman, Patricia Pratt aged 37, "I got real mad at him one time for staring at me."

One December night, Pratt decided to sit down with him.

"I felt sorry for him." She said.

Although his staring had angered her at first, her attitude had softened. He had become a familiar face in Y-B's over the weeks, and a few of the regulars eventually had caught on to his problem. Pratt knew why he behaved as he did.

"I found out he was deaf."

He didn't talk because he didn't know how. He could emit some intelligible sound, low and dense – "Mama" and "Mario" – but he'd never uttered words strung together.

Whether in the bar or out of it, he looked very isolated. He didn't know sign language and couldn't read lips; he was illiterate. Enveloped in silence since birth, never able to share his thoughts, to absorb or question ideas, he lived each day inside himself, a loner, learning what he could by watching other people.

It didn't take long for Pratt to grasp the extent of his disability. He could print his name in a child's scrawl. But except for crude drawings and simple hand gestures, he couldn't communicate.

"I was trying to teach him a little sign language," said Pratt, who once considered training to be an interpreter for the deaf and had read a book on the subject. "I don't know nothing but the basics: 'good boy,' 'good girl,' 'thank you,' 'you're welcome.'..." With Martinez, she realized the difficulty of conveying even the simplest abstract word concepts to a man as removed from language as he was.

"I didn't teach him much," she said.

Oswaldo Martinez was born in 1971 and came of age amid the chaos of El Salvador's brutal 12–year civil war, when death squads roamed the country. One of nine siblings, he grew up in squalor, toiling in sugar-cane fields beside his mother, who lost her husband to a grenade blast. Martinez never attended school and, except for his name and a few small words, he could not read or write.

A scene from El Salvador's bloody 12-year war showing victims from the much feared Death Squads. Martinez grew up in this era; the war preventing any form of education

155

Two of his brothers, Mario and Santiago, came to Virginia before him, each with a valid work permit. One found a job in construction, the other at a restaurant, in a part of the peninsula with a small but fast-growing Hispanic community. Bustling development in James City County (population 54,000) and a hospitality industry fuelled by Busch Gardens and Colonial Williamsburg had drawn Latino workers of several nationalities – immigrants generically labelled "Mexicans" by some in the county, which is 82 percent white.

Midway down the peninsula, Route 60 becomes Pocahontas Trail, lined with Trailer parks named Country Village, Heritage, Windy Hill – and Whispering Pines, where Binger was killed. Mario and Santiago Martinez rented trailers in Windy Hill, behind a parcel of drab storefronts that includes Y-B's, and lived there quietly with their families – until their brother Oswaldo arrived from El Salvador.

Asked how Oswaldo managed the journey to Virginia, Mario Martinez shrugged "We don't know," he said, speaking briefly outside his trailer on Beckie Lane, where Oswaldo stayed. He said his newly arrived brother, who showed up by surprise, was a nuisance – coming and going at all hours of the night, smoking cigarettes and swilling beer in the trailer. Although they did not want him, the brothers could not throw him out so it was decided that Oswaldo would move out and live in a shed in the yard.

The shed, resting on cinder blocks, became his little apartment, a 6-by-7-foot plywood box with a peaked ceiling seven feet high. Martinez, no stranger to hardship, found it liveable. Water and electricity came from the trailer. An air conditioner cooled him and a small camp stove gave him heat. He slept on a mattress, kept his meagre belongings in a pint-size dresser and showered in a tiny stall.

As for his day-labour wages, there was a country tavern close by where he could spend them.

By the end of the year, weeks after he began showing up in Y-B's, he was still just "Mexican guy" to most people, including bartender Parks, who noticed him in the booth by the restrooms on the night of Sunday January 2.

Jo Ann Johnson, 60, and other regulars saw him in the bar then, too, in baggy jeans and a light-coloured sweat shirt.

"He kept going in and out" of the tavern, Johnson recalled. "And he kept staring at me. And I told people, I said, 'I'm really getting nervous. He's just staring and staring'... He seemed very fidgety, very hyped or whatever. And he was going in and out, in and out..."

Sometime before 7.40 p.m., he went out and didn't come back that night.

Not long after the killing, Oswaldo Martinez found a social life in Y-B's.

It began one night when the cleaner wanted to mop near the man's booth and gestured for him to get up. "So we waved to him, you know, 'C'mon, sit with us,'" said Joan Specht, 54, who knew by then that he was deaf.

He seemed uncomfortable at first, sitting with the others like an appendage, his eyes darting around the table, watching lips move. Specht, who carries a tattered little notebook, printed "Your name" and showed it to him. He scrawled, "Oswaldo Martinez," which was pretty much all he could read or write. And then he just sat there, smiling occasionally at the conversations he couldn't hear.

As weeks passed, though, he loosened up, and the regulars could tell he enjoyed their company. He'd sit

157

with one small group or another and buy a round when his turn came.

"A very nice guy, very nice," said Tom Cail. "Oswaldo had a lot of friends in here after he started meeting all of us."

Six weeks after the killing, James City County police chief Stan Stout called a meeting.

With the investigation not producing any results, he assembled his detectives in their squad room, along with patrol officers who worked the stretch of Pocahontas Trail where the girl had been killed. They were going to watch a DVD. Before Binger's death, the company that owned Millers Mart had installed digital security cameras in the store, but no-one working in the mini-mart or for the county police could work out how to download images from the system onto a DVD.

After frustrating delays, police had finally managed to download the video. Now, in the squad room, looking at images from 2 January on a screen, the officers studied the faces of Millers Mart customers in the hours before Binger was attacked. The detectives wanted names for the faces – these were people in the vicinity of a homicide. More than a dozen patrol officers peered at the screen, searching for people they knew from their beats. Afternoon became evening on the DVD as hours passed in the squad room. The officers watched customers come and go, the digital images crisp and in colour. Then the video time counter reached 7.42 p.m.

Stout was sipping a Coke, leaning on a desk, when on the screen a man walked into Millers Mart in baggy jeans and a light-coloured sweat shirt and headed for a drinks cooler. In the instant before anyone spoke, the detectives leaned toward the video, riveted by what they saw.

Then someone said, "That's that Mexican guy from the bar."

"Freeze that!" someone shouted

Stout, turned to Gibbs, and Gibbs, staring at the screen, said yeah, that's the cooler the dog liked.

They watched, amazed.

"What the (expletive) is that in his hand?" someone asked.

Gibbs put the video on a smaller screen and enhanced it, focusing on a 20-ounce bottle the man had taken from the cooler. Detectives craned in, reading the label: Minute Maid, Strawberry Passion. Stout thought of the plastic juice bottle in the evidence box in the property room.

He sent an officer out to look at the bottle and turned his attention back to the video.

A different camera showed the man in baggy jeans pacing in front of the store with his drink – about the time Binger would have been cutting through the parking lot. To the detectives, he seemed anxious, stirred up, hyped.

Then the officer reported back from the property room: item No. 4, the plastic bottle standing upright near the body, almost full, was Minute Maid, Strawberry Passion, 20 ounce.

Bingo!

The detectives still had work to do, but after seeing the video, all their energy was focused in one direction. Except for a drunken-driving arrest here in early 2004, Martinez had no police record in the United States and the FBI found no official reports of sexual assaults or other crimes by him in El Salvador. Police wondered how he managed to fool the police and others with his driving licence and other identification at the time of his arrest for driving under the influence.

Oswaldo Martinez

The police needed something else besides the video that would link Martinez to the killing. They needed DNA.

In their minds, the police could visualise what happened that night. Martinez, standing outside Millers Mart, had seen Binger crossing the parking area behind the store and followed her in the dark to the Whispering Pines entrance, where he put down the bottle of strawberry-flavoured Minute Maid he had just bought. He jumps on her from behind, his arm squeezing the girl's neck, cutting off air, his open palm pressed against her mouth and nose, stifling her. The girl reaches behind with her left hand, the one that had skin under the fingernails, and scratches him somewhere. He rapes and then kills her, and runs away after arranging the body in a crucifix.

But, in the dark, he can't find his juice bottle or maybe, he forgets about it.

They sent the bottle to the state crime laboratory for DNA tests; they came back matching the saliva on the bottle to the semen in the dead girl and the skin under the fingernails. The bottle definitely belonged to the killer, and the number on the bottle showed it had been one of those in the machine in Millers Mart. Now they needed to match the saliva to the man.

They had enough evidence to support a search warrant application for hair and saliva samples from

Martinez but police worried that he would not stay around. He might run back to El Salvador and disappear.

Before the police could decide about the DNA samples, two of the investigators, Jake Rice and Rich Schugeld, walked into Y-B's late Tuesday afternoon, 15 February, and saw Martinez sitting at the bar, snipping a 12-ounce Bud. They called the owner Yvonne Belliveau aside and told her what they would like her to do. She understood the reason for the request.

Just then, as if on cue, Martinez downed the last of his Bud and got up, gesturing to the bartender that he was going out for smokes. He headed for Millers Mart.

As she had been told to do, Belliveau carefully picked up Martinez's empty Bud bottle and carried it to the kitchen. Rice joined her there and slipped the prize into an evidence bag. After locking the bottle in his car trunk, he was back in the booth with Schugeld, waiting for lunch, when Martinez came through the door and returned to his stool. The two detectives watched him order another beer with his hands. And then they ate their sandwiches.

Two days later, a DNA report said the saliva on the Budweiser bottle matched the semen and the fingernail skin. Martinez went to jail that night after police roused him out of bed at 3 a.m.

The arrest warrant was based on evidence from the hound going to the drinks cooler, the video showing Martinez getting a bottle from the cooler, the DNA from the bottle in the evidence room, and the photo that Pat Murray photo had taken of Martinez outside his shed early in the investigation, when "the Mexican guy" was just an odd little man in a bar-room booth whose name the police wanted to know.

They hadn't bothered to look at the photo then – it was just something to have available if they needed it. Not until they were about to arrest Martinez did they call up his image on the digital camera. And they saw what Murray hadn't noticed in the dark outside the shed, three nights after the killing.

"An abrasion on the lower left side of his face," they wrote. "Closer examination of this abrasion revealed that the flesh had been taken off his face, like a deep scratch."

And in Y-B's, among his friends, there was disbelief.

"He never gave us any kind of sign, no indication at all," Cail said.

"I thought they were just trying to pin this murder because he's deaf," Pratt said. "I still have a hard time believing it."

Unfortunately for the police and the District Attorney's Office, their problems were just beginning. Because of Oswaldo Martinez's lack of education and inability to communicate, it is possible the case would never come to trial.

Beau Webb, one of Martinez's attorneys, said he thinks a trial is out of the question for a least a few years because of his client's inability to communicate and assist in his defence, as required by law.

"We're dealing with a guy who doesn't have any base of linguistics. He doesn't have a grammar system – it's like teaching a baby," Webb told a news conference.

Anne Coughlin, a professor at the University Of Virginia School Of Law, said a judge presiding over a capital murder trial for Martinez would have difficulty balancing the community's right to have justice served with Martinez's right to due process.

"We lock people up, but we tell them why," Miss Coughlin said. "He doesn't know what's going to happen to him or when."

Oswaldo Martinez's right to a fair trial requires communication ability beyond his being able to say when or where something happened, Miss Coughlin said. He must be capable of understanding the advantages and disadvantages of entering a guilty plea, for example.

Martinez, who lacks formal sign language skills, is being held at Central State Hospital.

"I've never had a case like it," said Edward W. Webb, sitting with Martinez's file in Virginia's Office of the Capital Defender in Norfolk. Webb said he doesn't know what his client did or didn't do along Pocahontas Trail that night seven months ago. He and Martinez are unable to discuss it.

That is the problem.

An accused criminal who cannot assist in his own defense – who cannot communicate in any meaningful way with his attorney – is legally incompetent to stand trial. The U.S. Supreme Court says so. A vast majority of such cases involve mentally ill defendants, but that's not the issue for Martinez. His claim is "linguistic incompetence."

Two Gallaudet University psychologists, who were not deaf, evaluated him at Webb's request and supported a defence motion asking a judge to rule him incompetent. In a second evaluation, due at McGinty's request, specialists at Virginia's Western State Hospital agreed that Martinez is unfit to stand trial. A court hearing on the issue is set for 9 August.

In Virginia, a capital defendant – one facing lethal injection or life in prison without parole if convicted – can be institutionalised indefinitely if found incompetent while treatment specialists work to "restore competence."

For Martinez, that would mean absorbing the first formal education of his life.

He would have to learn words – what they are, what they signify – and become proficient enough at sign language to work with his lawyer. The process could take years and could prove fruitless, depending on his aptitude and willingness to learn, exerts said. What would be Martinez's incentive to learn? Eventually he could leave a hospital for jail, stand trial for murder and possibly be executed.

"The success rate for this type of thing evidently is not terribly high," Webb said.

Legal experts predict that the Oswaldo Martinez case would become as famous as the Donald Lang case[2]. Lang is still confined to a Chicago treatment centre over 40 years since he allegedly killed a prostitute. The case has been the subject of books and a TV movie titled "Dummy".

---

[2] Reported in *Deaf Murder Casebook* by the same author, published in 1999.